CHASING
HELICITY

THROUGH
the
STORM

Also by Ginger Zee

Chasing Helicity—Force of Nature
Chasing Helicity—Into the Wind

CHASING
HELICITY

THROUGH
the
STORM

GINGER Zee

𝕯𝖎𝖘𝖓𝖊𝖞 · HYPERION

Los Angeles   New York

First Edition, April 2020
10 9 8 7 6 5 4 3 2 1
Printed in the United States of America
FAC-020093-20066

This book is set in Adobe Caslon Pro, Helvetica Neue LT Pro/Monotype,
Core Circus, Mrs Eaves OT/Fontspring
Designed by Tyler Nevins

ISBN 978-1-368-00218-9

Library of Congress Control Number: 2019955969

Visit www.DisneyBooks.com

For Dawn, my scientist mom who inspired me to dream without limits. I love you.

CHASING HELICITY

THROUGH the STORM

Helicity tilted her head back and drank in the beauty of the night sky. From her perch high atop the Bolivar Peninsula lighthouse, the stars looked close enough to touch. The crescent moon bathed her face, the platform, and the thick glass of the lighthouse beacon in its pale light. The air was so still, she could hear waves gently lapping down below. In that moment, it was easy to imagine that the hurricane was gone for good.

It wasn't. And Helicity knew that without looking

at a radar or satellite image of the hurricane—she knew exactly where she was. That open sky was the hurricane's eye. Seen from a satellite, it would look like a small dark hole in the middle of an immense rotating disk of gray-white clouds. From Helicity's perspective, towering dark clouds encircled the patch of clear sky. She imagined it had the stadium effect, as that cloud phenomenon was called, because it resembled an open-domed sports arena—but she couldn't see all the way up; it was too dark. She'd seen video footage of it before, but nothing compared to witnessing it firsthand. It left her feeling awed.

Awed, and very, very uneasy. Those dark clouds made up the hurricane's eye wall, the most destructive part of the storm. Powerful thunderstorms, fueled by moisture sucked up from the warm Gulf of Mexico, could potentially dump several more inches of rain on the peninsula, drowning land that was already severely flooded. Damaging wind would most certainly return to pummel her and everything at the coast for a hundred miles. That wind could reach speeds of more than 150 miles per hour—twice as fast as a locomotive and every bit as life-threatening to anything in its path. The conditions might even spin up a tornado.

Helicity had been caught in a tornado once before. She wanted no part of a second experience.

And now the back edge of that eye wall was edging toward the Bolivar coastline. Toward the lighthouse. Toward her.

A light breeze thick with humidity teased her hair. She'd have to retreat to the lower deck in a few minutes. The lighthouse's brick walls were falling apart in places, but the ironclad landmark had stood strong in the face of hurricanes before. Helicity trusted it would protect her during this storm.

Not that she had any other options. The lighthouse was the only structure still standing for miles.

Even so, she was reluctant to return down below. Outside, the air smelled fresh, and the moon cast enough light for her to see. Inside, the water pooling at the bottom of the lighthouse reeked of raw sewage, gasoline, and her own vomit, plus other substances she couldn't identify and wasn't sure she wanted to. She had no source of light or means of communication, not since one of her cell phones shattered on the spiral staircase and the other died in the seawater below.

Inside, she would be isolated. Cut off from everything and everyone. Completely, utterly alone.

Stop it, Helicity. Thinking like that doesn't help, so just . . . stop.

As she turned toward the trapdoor, a flicker of light caught her eye. She blinked, sure she had imagined it. But then it came again. A small boat slipped into view from behind the ruins of a toppled house. A lone figure sat by the outboard motor.

Her heart skipped a beat. *Sam.*

There could be only one reason Sam Levesque was out there: he'd found her note explaining that she'd gone to the lighthouse to search for her brother, Andy. Now, like a knight in shining armor, he was coming to rescue her, the damsel in distress trapped in the tower.

Except I'm no damsel, and he's the one who will need saving if he doesn't get to shelter now! Warring emotions—fury at Sam's recklessness, fear for his safety, and the tiniest spark of joy that he'd come for her despite the risks—bubbled up inside her. Then the person shouted.

"Scout! Here, Scout! I've got a treat for you! Where are you, girl?"

Helicity's eyes widened. *That's not Sam. It's a man looking for a dog!*

She understood the impulse to rescue a loved one, human or animal. Her need to help Andy had driven her to the lighthouse. But she had chased after her brother long before the hurricane hit. Why was this man out now, when the worst of the storm was about to engulf them?

She gasped with sudden understanding. "He doesn't know what's coming!"

She'd heard stories of people who mistook the eye of the hurricane for the end of the storm. Too often, those stories ended in tragedy.

Not this time! She shot a savage glare at the clouds looming overhead, then cupped her hands into a megaphone. "Hey! Hey, mister! The hurricane isn't over! Find shelter *now*!"

The flashlight beam continued to play over piles of debris. She cursed. He hadn't heard her. Maybe the wind gusts, more frequent and stronger now, had snatched away her warning, or the boat's motor had drowned out her shouts. Or maybe she was just too far away and too high up for her voice to carry down to him. She tried again, yelling until her throat felt raw. But the boat kept motoring along, the light moving in sweeping arcs as the man called for his dog.

Overhead, the eye wall was slowly swallowing the moon. A sense of helplessness boiled up inside her. *If he doesn't get out of here—*

The boat suddenly looped around. The motor revved, and the man sped off. Helicity sagged with relief as she watched him disappear into the darkness. Saying a silent prayer for his safety, she hurried to the trapdoor and climbed down the ladder. She pulled the hatch shut behind her with a solid thud, sealing herself inside.

And not a moment too soon. As if someone had flicked a switch, the gusting wind grew to a freight-train howl. The clouds let loose a downpour that pounded on the platform above her head. A deafening clap of thunder ripped through the air, its vibrations reverberating through her body.

Helicity dropped down on all fours and crawled through the pitch dark until she came to a wall. Her fingertips touched wetness. Rainwater was streaming down the whitewashed bricks. She pressed her lips to the widest rivulet, grateful for the drink.

Blam! Something slammed against the outside of the lighthouse with such force, her mouth jarred against the bricks. She jerked back, tasting blood instead of water, every muscle tense, waiting for a second blow. When none came, she edged forward and resumed drinking. The water stung the cuts on her lips, but she didn't care. She drank until she could hold no more, then inched to a dry section of floor and sat down with a tremulous sigh. Knees sagging to either side and hands resting limply in her lap, she tipped her head back and let her heavy eyelids droop closed.

Up until then, she'd managed to keep the worst of her fears at bay. But now her guard was down. Anxiety crept in and took root. For the man in the boat, for herself, and especially for those she loved most in the world.

Mom. Dad. Andy. Her stomach clenched as she imagined her frantic parents. But it was Andy whom she feared for the most.

Sam had found him; she'd learned that much before their phone call had been cut off. She clung to the hope that the two had made it off the peninsula before the hurricane hit. But her brother had worse obstacles ahead. Much, much worse.

Tears pricked her eyes. Just a few short months ago, Andy had been a star athlete with a bright future. More importantly, he was a kind soul with a warm, loving heart. Addiction to painkillers had stolen that Andy from her, had changed him into a moody, shifty-eyed stranger who resorted to petty thievery to feed his drug habit. She'd been devastated when she found out, and furious with herself for not recognizing what was happening to him sooner. She still didn't understand how he'd let addiction take over his life, but that didn't matter. What did was making sure he got the chance to be whole again.

Get him somewhere safe, Sam, she pleaded silently. *And Andy . . . just hang on.*

Her hand fumbled for a pair of charms on her necklace. The golden lightning bolt belonged to her friend and mentor, Lana McElvoy. Trey Valdez, a sweet boy she'd met just a few weeks earlier, had given her the tiny bottle containing a single piece of silver-blue dolphin confetti as a going-away gift the afternoon before. He'd given her something else, too: her first kiss.

A second kiss had followed, but not from Trey. From Sam. Trey's kiss had been tentative but nice, like him. But Sam's . . . *Oh.* That electrifying moment was seared into her memory forever. The way he stopped her talking with a gentle finger to her lips. How he traced his finger to her chin and tilted her head. How she couldn't breathe when his ice-blue eyes locked with her sea-green ones. When he closed the distance between them. When his impossibly soft lips touched hers.

Warmth bloomed inside her at the memory, and though it felt wrong to be happy, she clung to the feeling. Let it spread until it chased all other emotions away. Still grasping the charms, she slid sideways down the bricks to the wooden floor, curled her legs in tight, and with the raging hurricane as her lullaby, drifted off into a dreamless sleep.

CHAPTER TWO

A single beam of sunlight roused Helicity from her slumber. She rolled to her back and groaned. Her body ached from lying on the hard, wooden floor. Her swollen lips were dry, and her stomach pinched with hunger, a reminder that she hadn't eaten in two days. When she sat up, small black dots danced before her eyes. Then her vision narrowed to a long tunnel.

"Oh, no, you don't, Dunlap," she croaked as she eased back down. "Absolutely no passing out."

She propped her feet high up on the wall to let the oxygen-rich blood flow to her brain. Eyes closed, she took slow, deep breaths, in through her nose and out through her mouth, waiting for her equilibrium to return to normal.

"Right. Let's try that again." She wasn't usually one to talk to herself, but the sound of her voice was oddly soothing in the intense quiet that had replaced the roaring wind and driving rain. She moved slower this time, first sitting and then getting to her hands and knees, pausing at each step. She licked her lips, alarmed at their dryness and the fact that her throat felt as if she'd swallowed sandpaper.

Relief washed through her when she spotted a few puddles scattered around the platform. She could survive without food for a week or more. Without water, though, she would become severely dehydrated in three days. Longer than that, and she might literally die of thirst.

She crawled from puddle to puddle, drinking each with eager sips until they were gone. She rested for a few minutes, gathering her strength to climb the ladder and push open the trapdoor.

Getting to the upper deck was vital. Many search-and-rescue missions started with air reconnaissance of the disaster site. Helicopters used to be the vehicle of choice, but more and more frequently, drones had become the first and primary surveillance tool. Small, unmanned, and remote-controlled, they could be deployed much faster and more safely than manned vehicles. Their high-definition cameras relayed important information about potential hazards to ground crews monitoring their feeds on computer screens. Some drones had sophisticated temperature sensors, too, that could zero in on missing persons. Like her.

There were no guarantees that drones sent out in this disaster would have those sensors, though. So, her best bet was to be where their cameras could spot her.

Blazing sunlight temporarily blinded her when she opened the trapdoor. She twisted her head away, scrambled up through the hatch, and collapsed on the upper deck.

It had been as silent as a tomb inside the lighthouse. Lying on the hot planks, her eyes slit against the sunlight, she became aware of sounds. The ear-piercing shriek of a seagull wheeling overhead, and the faint thump and whoosh of waves washing against the peninsula's shoreline. The sobering snap and crack of debris as water pushed and pulled at the shattered, drowned remnants of people's lives.

Then a single mournful note sliced through the air.

A dog, her brain registered. *That's a dog whining. And it's nearby.*

She crawled to the railing and peered over the edge. Standing on a slab of broken decking down below was a small brown-and-white dog with stubby little legs. Whenever the dog moved, the decking tilted, pitching him off his paws and eliciting another desperate whine. The poor thing looked so lost, sounded so pitiable, that she knew she couldn't leave it there to suffer.

"Don't you worry," she murmured, her voice raspy with thirst. "I'm coming to get you."

But she paused with her foot on the ladder's top rung. What if a drone buzzed by while she was inside the lighthouse?

Sunlight reflecting off the lighthouse's glass beacon gave her an idea. *A signal. I need to leave a signal that I'm here.* The beacon itself was the obvious choice, except it hadn't been functional for years. Even if it had worked, she wouldn't have had a clue how to operate it.

Then she glanced down at her shirt. Vibrant pink with I HEART BOLIVAR in bold black print across the front, the shirt had been in the two-dollar bargain bin at a local souvenir shop. Her best friend, Mia, had doubled over with laughter when she'd seen Helicity carrying it to the checkout counter. "Hot pink? Seriously?" she'd managed to gasp. "And it's huge!"

Helicity bought it anyway. She liked oversize T-shirts, especially Andy's castoffs, and the price was right.

She gave silent thanks for that brilliant Day-Glo pink now. She pulled the shirt over her head, beyond caring that she was only wearing a sports bra and shorts now. She started to tie the shirt to the railing, then changed her mind and tugged it over the beacon instead. It was a tight fit, and the sleeves stuck out on either side, making the old glass fixture look like a headless, limbless shop mannequin. But that hot-pink shirt made the perfect signal: easy to spot and obviously put there by a person.

That's all I can do for now, she thought as she returned

to the trapdoor. *That, and hope a drone or a copter comes by soon.*

Leaving the hatch open for light and fresh air, she began her descent down the spiral staircase. She moved with extreme caution. Yesterday, the railing had pulled free from the wall and sent her plummeting to the ground below. She'd woken with a lump on her forehead that still throbbed with pain.

As she neared the bottom, she called out to the dog. "I'm coming, little fella! You hear me, boy? I'm coming!"

The dog replied with short barks that made her smile. That smile faded, though, when she came to the contaminated floodwaters that had seeped into the lighthouse. The smell was overpowering, forcing her to breathe through her mouth so she didn't gag. The knee-deep water was likely teeming with harmful bacteria and other biohazards. She knew sea creatures suffered from skin diseases and worse afflictions after being exposed to such toxins. A long scratch on her arm, given to her by an angry owl, had already been submerged in that cesspool once. A second dousing doubled her chances of infection.

Doesn't matter. Because no way I'm letting that dog suffer.

She lowered herself into the filthy water and slogged to the door. When she tugged it open, the dog swiveled to look at her. *Scout,* the tag on its collar read.

"You're that man's dog, aren't you?" she murmured. "Hey, Scout. Here, boy. I mean, girl." She pitched her voice low and soft, the same tone she had recently used to soothe a stranded dolphin and that always calmed her horse, Raven. Still murmuring, her eyes never leaving Scout, she reached forward and grabbed the edge of the decking to steady it.

Pain, sudden and intense, shot up her arm. She'd spiked her palm on a rusty nail!

"No! Ah! No!" she yelped.

Scout scurried backward, away from her. The decking rocked violently with the dog's movement. The nail dug in deeper. She yelped again and with one quick upward jerk, wrenched her hand free. The decking tilted again, and Scout lost her footing and toppled over the edge.

"No!" Ignoring the blood dripping from her hand,

Helicity splashed through a stagnant pool of water to where the dog had fallen.

Scout's small furry form lay slumped over a rotted two-by-four, half-submerged in water. She wasn't moving.

No-no-no-no-no! Helicity's mind screamed. She dropped to her knees in the water, no longer caring that she was putting her own health at risk. "No," she whispered. "No."

Suddenly, Scout gave a snort. Wild-eyed, she struggled to stand. Helicity swept the shivering wet body up in her arms.

"You're okay, I got you, you're okay," she babbled. "And I'm not going to let you go."

Scout stilled in Helicity's embrace. Helicity lurched to her feet and made her way back inside the lighthouse. Clutching the dog to her shoulder with her bloody hand, she used the other to haul them up the spiral staircase. They'd just reached the ladder when she heard a strange sound, like a mosquito, only much louder.

Louder, and man-made.

A drone!

"Wait!" Throwing caution to the wind, Helicity scrambled up the ladder. Her wet sneaker slipped on a rung, and she and Scout nearly fell. She regained her balance and fumbled her way through the hatch.

Just in time to see the drone buzzing away.

CHAPTER THREE

"I t saw us, right? Or at least my T-shirt! No way its camera could have missed that!"

Helicity sank down next to the beacon with Scout still pressed to her chest. The little dog licked her face, then gazed at her with soulful eyes. Helicity felt her tension ease a bit and ruffled Scout's damp ears. When she caught sight of her bloody palm and the stain it had left on the dog's fur, she blanched. She set Scout down, tugged her shirt from the beacon, and wrapped her hand to stanch the flow. The pain was

19

fierce, but she could wiggle her fingers, so at least the nail hadn't pierced anything vital. Infection was still a threat. And the nail had been rusty. . . .

Scout nosed her gently, then settled onto her lap as if she knew there was nothing else to do but wait. Helicity stroked the dog's head a few times, then shaded her eyes and searched the sky for the drone.

The sun, such a welcome sight earlier, now made her miserable. It beat down on her exposed skin, turning it pink. It dried the filthy water on her legs, torso, and arms to a crusty scum that made her feel itchy all over. Any lingering puddles she and Scout might have drunk had long since evaporated.

That's when she realized Scout was right: there was nothing else to do but wait. Wait, and hope.

The baking-hot platform slowly drained her energy. Her thoughts narrowed onto one thing: water. Clean, pure water, flowing over her cracked lips, through the desert of her mouth, down her parched throat. Warm, sudsy water cascading through her hair and over her body. Lake Michigan's icy water shocking the breath from her lungs and landscaping her skin with goose bumps. As minutes ticked by, her longing for water grew until she would have done anything—*anything*—to get her hands on some.

This is how Andy felt.

That truth hit her like a ton of bricks. *He wanted those painkillers more than anything else in his life. Football, friends, college*—she swallowed hard—*me, none of it mattered enough for him to stop.*

She knew her longing for water wasn't the same as what Andy experienced. With one long drink, one warm shower, her need would be quenched and soon forgotten. Not Andy. The more he fed his addiction, the greater his need to feed it would grow, until it was all-consuming. And when that happened, the Andy she loved so much would be lost forever.

A faint buzzing sound cut through her dismal thoughts. Her eyes flew open. She lurched to her knees, dumping Scout unceremoniously from her lap as a dark, insect-like shape sailed through the air toward them.

"Here!" She pulled herself up by the beacon and waved her shirt-wrapped hand frantically. "I'm right here!"

The drone buzzed closer to the lighthouse, hovered,

and released a small sack onto the platform. When Helicity saw what was inside, she almost wept. Two plastic bottles of water, sweating with condensation and still cold to the touch. With trembling fingers, she cranked off a cap.

Nothing had ever tasted so good as that first clean, clear sip. She was so focused on the sensation of the liquid trickling down her parched throat that she didn't notice the cell phone inside the sack until it started ringing. She withdrew it and tapped Accept.

"Hello?" a woman said. "Hello, can you hear me?"

"Yes!" Helicity cried. "Yes, I can hear you! My name is Helicity Dunlap and—"

"Helicity!" A second voice broke in, also female and choked with emotion. "Oh, my God, Helicity, darling!"

"Mom? *Mom!*" Helicity slumped against the beacon, the phone cradled to her ear, her eyes pinned on the camera mounted to the hovering drone. "It's me, Mom. It's me! Can you see me?"

"Oh, my sweet girl, yes, I see right here on the monitor! Are you okay? What a stupid question. Of course you aren't, not after what you have been through. . . ."

Her mother's voice trailed off into sobs that echoed through the phone.

The first woman came back on. "Helicity, we're sending help from the National Guard, but we need to know if you need urgent medical attention so we can have the right equipment on board."

Helicity told the woman about her hand, that it and the scratch on her arm had been exposed to contaminated water, and that she had probably suffered a concussion from the fall down the spiral staircase. "I'm dehydrated, too, though the water you sent is helping. Oh, and I'm not alone! I found a dog named Scout." She quickly explained about the man in the boat.

"Understood," the woman said. "We'll be on the lookout for the dog's owner. In the meantime, we're sending someone to get you. Give us half an hour, then head to the bottom of the lighthouse. Can you do that?"

"Yes!"

"Good. And, Helicity, wait inside when you get there. It's too dangerous outside."

The phone changed hands again. "Darling, they have to send the drone on to survey another location, but I'm going to stay on the line with you as long as I can," her mother said. "Cell service is spotty, though, because the hurricane knocked down several towers. So I might lose you. Not *lose* you lose you," she added, her tone so stricken that Helicity had to smile.

"I know you're not going to lose me, Mom. But man oh, man, am I glad you found me." She started to ask about Andy and Sam and her father. But the call abruptly cut off. She tried dialing back, but the connection failed every time.

"It's okay, though, Scout." She poured the rest of the water from the bottle into a puddle for the dog, then opened the second one. As she sipped, she wrapped the fingers of her injured hand around her necklace charms. "Because they're on their way."

She monitored the cell-phone clock for the next half hour. When time was up, she gathered Scout into her arms again. Midway down the spiral staircase, she glanced at the roost of the owl that she had last seen the day before.

A casualty of the hurricane that no one but me will ever know or care about.

Downstairs, her mood lifted when she heard the

growl of an approaching vehicle. A large SUV plowed through the stagnant water, sending up a shower of dirt-brown waves, and slowed to a stop near the lighthouse. A rugged-looking older man wearing a bright yellow jacket, black waterproof pants, rubber boots, and a dingy white hard hat swung out of the passenger seat.

"Pee-yew! What a stink!" He waved a hand under his nose as he strode to Helicity's side, his deep Texas twang echoing through the lighthouse. He tilted his head and grinned. "My name's Steve. Heard you might like to get on out of here."

Helicity blinked back sudden tears. "You—you heard right," she quavered.

"Then let's make it happen, Cap'n!" With a cheerful "Up-si-daisy!" as his only warning, Steve scooped her into his arms as if she were a toddler. "Two for the price of one," he joked, looking at Scout nestled in her arms. "Not a bad day's work. Now, what say we get you to your momma?"

Helicity buried her face against his broad shoulder. "I say yes. A big, huge *yes*!"

CHAPTER FOUR

I n the SUV, Steve draped a blanket over Helicity's shoulders. While the driver pointed them back toward the mainland, Steve disinfected and dressed her wounds, examined the lump on her forehead, shone a penlight in her eyes, and finally handed her an energy drink and a chocolate-covered protein bar. "Take it slow with those. Your stomach's not ready for a full meal, and we don't want everything that goes in to come back up again."

It took great willpower to nibble the bar, not gobble

it. But as the SUV slowly moved east toward the mainland, Helicity lost her appetite. She'd seen the hurricane's devastation from high above and thought she was prepared to see it up close.

She wasn't. The debris-infested wasteland whirred past the SUV's windows like a dystopian horror film on fast forward. Abandoned cars covered in drying muck. A refrigerator half-buried in sand. The charred remains of a house like a massive gaping mouth with blackened teeth. Clothing ripped into rags, broken televisions, a mulched mess of magazines and books, dead fish, and slimy ropes of seaweed—the peninsula's landscape was rotting beneath a plague of trash and garbage. Even the lighthouse had suffered. A section of its iron plating now bore a large dent—from being struck by the flagpole, she guessed when she saw the pole lying at an angle below the dent. She touched her lips, remembering the jarring impact that shook the lighthouse the night before.

Helicity's heart broke when they neared the turnoff where the Beachside Bed and Breakfast stood. *Where the turnoff used to be*, she amended silently. *Where the Beachside used to stand.*

Like so many other seaside houses, the place she'd called home that summer had been shoved off its pilings by the powerful storm surge and hurricane-whipped waves. Now it was nothing more than a heaving heap of debris listing in a sea of sand. Glass glinted from the wreckage. From the picture window through which she'd watched a thunderstorm? The tip jar she and Mia had slowly filled—and that Andy had emptied one horrible night? The glass-and-wood-framed photo Sam had taken of the lighthouse? Those things were gone now. Those, and so much more, too.

Oh, Suze. She bit her lip and pulled Scout closer. Mia's aunt would be crushed when she saw the ruins of her beloved bed-and-breakfast.

After what felt like an eternity, the SUV pulled into a parking lot next to the search-and-rescue unit's makeshift command center. Mrs. Dunlap burst out the trailer door. Helicity shoved Scout into Steve's waiting hands, tore open the car door, and flung herself into her mother's tight embrace. They rocked in each other's arms, both trembling, her mother tearfully whispering the same reassurances Helicity had babbled to Scout. "You're okay. You're safe. I've got you. And I'm not letting go."

An ambulance roared up, and Steve shooed them both into the back, where a paramedic was waiting. As Helicity settled onto a stretcher, Steve waved Scout's paw to her and called, "I'll do everything I can to find this little pooch's owner!" Then he shut the ambulance doors, and they took off.

Moving with brisk efficiency, the paramedic hung an IV bag that dripped fluids and antibiotics through a tube into Helicity's arm. "You need anything for pain?"

"No!" her mother interjected vehemently. "Absolutely no painkillers!"

The paramedic held up his hands as if defending himself. "I wasn't suggesting anything stronger than acetaminophen. Not when a concussion is suspected."

Helicity was as startled by her mother's reaction as he was. Understanding dawned when she read the anguish etched in her face, saw the deep, dark circles beneath her eyes. "You know," she whispered. "About Andy."

Her mother's mouth worked. "Sam told us everything."

"Sam?" Helicity started to sit up. The paramedic gently but firmly pushed her back down. "He—they—Mom, where are they? Are they all right? Is Andy okay?"

Her mother leaned forward heavily, elbows on knees, and scrubbed her face with her hands. "Andy . . ." She shook her head. "He's in trouble, Hel. But he'd be so much worse if not for Sam."

She took a deep breath, then told Helicity what had happened after Sam left her at the Beachside to fuel up his car. "It took him forever because of the traffic and the long lines at the pumps. When he got back to the Beachside, you were gone. He was frantic until he found your note. He went after you immediately. Partway to the lighthouse, he saw Andy stumbling down a side road. He tried to get him into the car. Andy resisted. Took a swing at him. He missed. Sam didn't."

Her mother touched her midsection to indicate where Sam's punch had landed on Andy. "Sam got him into the backseat and then started for the lighthouse again." She took Helicity's hand. "He couldn't get there. The hurricane's outer bands had already torn at the power lines, and sparks were flying from transformers. Something—a propane tank from a grill, they think—exploded and set a house on fire. The authorities refused to let Sam pass."

Helicity flashed back to the burned-out home they'd driven by in the SUV. *I must have been unconscious when the explosion happened*, she thought. But in her mind's eye she could see the fireball and the flames licking at the sky, feel the scorching heat, and picture the windblown sparks floating through the air. Those sparks could have easily ignited spilled oil or gasoline, causing another fire or explosion. She shivered, understanding why the authorities had forced Sam to turn back.

"Sam would have disobeyed their orders, except . . ." She shook her head, unable to go on.

"Andy," Helicity guessed. "He started to show signs of withdrawal, didn't he?"

The paramedic shot her a sharp glance, then busied himself with her IV.

"Sam thinks so," her mother answered. "And that left him with a horrible choice: force his way past the authorities and possibly risk all three of your lives trying to get to you, or get Andy to safety and get him the help he needed."

Helicity was quiet. The sway and bump of the ambulance reminded her of how the lighthouse had rocked during the worst of the hurricane. How would Andy have fared if he'd been trapped there while experiencing the early stages of withdrawal? Would he have even stayed, or would his addiction have driven him to take his chances in the storm? She shuddered to imagine what would have happened then.

"Where is Andy?" she asked.

"A treatment facility near the hospital we are going to now." Her mother told her the name of the place.

"That's an excellent rehab center." The paramedic lifted his chin and returned their gazes. "Forgive me for sticking my nose in where it doesn't belong, but I have experience with addiction. Believe me when I say your boy will be in very good hands there. And if you ever have any questions"—he fumbled in his back pocket and withdrew a business card—"just call or text. Anytime, day or night. I mean that."

Helicity's mother slipped the card into her purse with a nod. They rode in silence for a while longer.

Then the ambulance turned a corner and slowed to a stop.

"We're here," the paramedic said when the back doors opened. "This is where I leave you, but remember: anytime, day or night." He smiled. "Don't take this the wrong way, Helicity, but I hope I never see you in my ambulance again."

"I hope you don't, either," someone outside the ambulance said.

Helicity's breath caught in her throat. This time when she sat up, the paramedic didn't stop her. Strong arms captured her in a tight embrace, and that's when she knew with absolute certainty that she was safe.

"Dad," she whispered. And again, even more softly: "Dad."

CHAPTER FIVE

Her father wanted to take Helicity to their hotel. But the hospital staff overrode him and admitted her. A doctor checked her wounds and tested her for concussion symptoms. Her test results were better than expected—no real dizziness, blurred vision, or problems with concentration—but he insisted she spend the night in the hospital for further observation, just to be safe.

"Rest," he added, "is the best cure for concussion. So, no strenuous activity, limit your screen time, and above all, see your doctor when you get home."

After a long, hot shower, Helicity slipped into bed. Thin and narrow as it was, the hospital mattress felt pillowy soft beneath her aching, bruised body. She used the last of her energy to kiss her parents, then fell fast asleep.

She awoke refreshed hours later. Refreshed, and ravenous. She pressed the call button attached to her bed, hoping to get something to eat.

"Well, it's about time." A lanky teenager with jet-black hair and piercing ice-blue eyes uncoiled himself from a chair. "I was getting tired of listening to you snore."

Helicity gasped with surprise. "Sam!"

Sam adjusted his retro concert T-shirt over his snug-fitting jeans. His boots thudded on the floor as he crossed the room to stand by her side. "Hey."

"Hey," she replied.

Helicity was suddenly keenly aware that underneath the scratchy hospital sheet, she wore nothing but the open-backed johnny the hospital had given her. She tried to finger-comb her hair, certain that it resembled a rat's nest. But with the thick bandage wrapped around her palm, she just made it worse. She gave an embarrassed laugh. "I bet I look—"

His hand darted out and captured hers. "You look great. Well, except for the ding mark on your forehead and the gouge on your arm and the stab wound in your palm and the swelling in your—your lips."

The way he stumbled over those last words made her blush to her roots. He dropped her hand like a hot potato and retrieved his chair. "So, um, how are you feeling?" he asked as he sat.

"Better," she said. "You?"

"Me? Oh, yeah, I'm good. I'm good."

"That's . . . good."

An awkward silence fell between them, then they both spoke at once.

"Sam, what you did for Andy—"

"I should never have left you—"

They broke off at the same time, then simultaneously said, "You first. No, you!"

Helicity started laughing. Chuckling, Sam inched his chair closer and recaptured her hand. "I was going to say that I should never have left you alone at the Beachside. It was stupid of me."

"No stupider than me staying behind instead of going with you," she argued. "And taking off for the lighthouse instead of waiting for you." She looked down at their clasped hands. "I heard you tried to come after me." She glanced up, caught him staring at her, and held his gaze. "Thank you."

Now it was his turn to flush. "If it wasn't for that explosion," he muttered, "I would have made it to the lighthouse."

"But instead, you saved Andy. And that means more to me than anything. Seriously."

Their conversation was interrupted by a nurse with a tray of breakfast food. She raised her eyebrows when she saw Sam. "You still here?" She set the tray down on a rolling table. "He's been in that chair for the last, what—three hours?" she told Helicity. "He didn't even turn on the TV. Most people do after fifteen minutes."

"I couldn't find the remote!" Sam protested.

The nurse sniffed. "You mean that little device on the stand next to your chair? Yeah, I can see how that might be difficult to spot." She maneuvered the table into position over Helicity's bed and removed the lid from a plate of scrambled eggs and toast. "You ask me, he just found something he liked watching better than morning talk shows or cartoons." She gave Helicity an elaborate wink, grinned at Sam, and trundled out.

Helicity and Sam looked at each other, then quickly looked away. Sam snatched up the remote, mumbling about catching up on news about the hurricane. While he clicked through channels, Helicity gave her breakfast her full concentration. But the eggs had grown cold and after three forkfuls, she pushed the plate away, lay back against the pillows, and glanced up at the television.

And did a double take. "Sam, turn it up! Turn it up!"

Sam bumped up the volume. "What is it?"

"Shhh!" Helicity hissed.

On the screen was the host of a morning talk show, an impeccably dressed woman with sleek auburn hair captured in a neat side bun. Sitting next to her on a sofa was an older man in jeans and a blue golf shirt. He was holding a little dog. "That's Scout!" Helicity cried.

"Who is, the guy or the dog?"

Helicity flapped her hand at Sam to tell him to be quiet.

The host turned a solemn face to the camera. "It will be days before we know the full extent of the damage left by the hurricane that devastated so many coastline communities around the Gulf of Mexico." Her expression softened. "But out of that catastrophe comes an uplifting and unlikely story of reunion." She turned to the man. "Charles Bainbridge, welcome and thank you for joining us this morning."

"Thank you for having me, Cheryl," the man replied.

When she heard the man's voice, Helicity's eyes widened with recognition. "He's the man in the boat! Oh, thank goodness, he's okay!"

"What boat? Who is that guy? Who's Scout?" Sam demanded.

Helicity shushed him again.

Cheryl leaned forward and gestured at the little dog. "Charles, tell us about Scout."

Charles cleared his throat. "Scout is an ESA—an emotional support animal. She helps my eight-year-old daughter, Tabitha, who suffers from bouts of anxiety."

"Helps how?" Cheryl prodded.

"She senses when Tabitha is on the verge of

emotional distress. As I understand it, many animals, dogs particularly, can pick up on physical changes in the human body that come with anxiety—accelerated heart rate, shortness of breath, that sort of thing. Scout responds to Tabitha's stress by comforting her with gentle licks, cuddling up close, and other affectionate gestures." Charles smiled. "Anyone who owns a dog or other loving pet knows what I'm talking about. With Scout by her side, Tabitha is better equipped to cope with her challenges. And that means she's a happier, healthier girl overall."

"But Scout wasn't by Tabitha's side during the hurricane, was she?" Cheryl's voice was full of concern.

Charles didn't answer right away. Instead, he buried his nose in Scout's fur. Scout twisted around and licked his face. With a jolt, Helicity remembered the little dog doing the same thing when they were together. She remembered, too, how that small, instinctual gesture had soothed her.

"Tabitha and I live in New Mexico. We'd come to Bolivar for a week's vacation." He gave a mirthless laugh. "Next time we'll check the weather predictions before leaving Albuquerque."

Cheryl nodded sympathetically. "Not much of a vacation, I'm afraid. So, what happened?"

"When it came time to evacuate, we couldn't find Scout," Charles replied. "We searched everywhere, but in the end, we had to leave her behind. When the storm calmed down, though, I went back to look for her. I know now it was foolish, that I was putting myself in danger, but . . . well, I'm a parent. I'd do anything for my daughter. But the clouds came back. The wind picked up. I had to return to Tabitha without Scout. When I walked into our hotel room empty-handed . . ." He trailed off, overcome.

Cheryl touched his knee lightly. "I have no doubt Tabitha understands. And besides, Scout found her way back to you after all!"

Charles brightened. "Yes, and that's why I'm so grateful to you for having me on today, Cheryl. I'm not here just to share my story. I came on your show because I want to thank the courageous girl who rescued Scout. From what I've been told, she risked her own well-being to save our dog. But of course, she didn't just save Scout. She saved Tabitha." He looked directly at the camera. "So, Helicity Dunlap, if you're out there watching, thank you. Thank you from the bottom of my heart."

Helicity had been listening raptly, touched by the man's story. Now she gulped, stunned at hearing her name. The show cut to a commercial then, and Sam hit the mute button.

"Wow, Fifteen. You're a hero."

She looked at him sharply, wondering if he was teasing her. But to her consternation, he looked impressed. "What? No, I'm not," she sputtered.

"He's right. You are." The nurse had returned in time to hear their exchange. She handed Helicity a dose of antibiotics and a cup of water. "And you might be a little bit famous soon, too." She jerked her chin at the television, where the program had resumed. "Cheryl Wiggins has been a big deal here in Texas for a while, and now she's making a name for herself nationwide. I wouldn't be surprised if that story gets picked up by other networks. And if it does, mark my words," she added as she headed out the door, "people are going to want to know more about the girl in the lighthouse."

Helicity stared after her, then drew the thin cotton

bedsheet up under her chin. Some people sought fame, she knew, but the idea of strangers probing into her life made her feel more vulnerable than her open-backed johnny. Not that she had any skeletons in her closet . . . except Andy.

As that thought struck her mind, Sam's phone rang, signaling an incoming video chat. He raised his eyebrows when he saw the caller's number. "I'm pretty sure this is for you, Fifteen."

He held the phone out to Helicity. For a split second, she feared the nurse's prediction had come true, that someone seeking information about her had somehow gotten hold of Sam's number. Then she saw who was calling and broke into a huge grin.

CHAPTER SIX

"**L**ana!"

Helicity's grin broadened when her men‐tor's image materialized on the tiny screen. Lana's face was pale and drawn, and her naturally curly blond hair had lost some of its bounce—the result of lying in a coma for weeks, Helicity assumed. But her eyes were bright, and her smile was as warm as ever. "Oh, man, Lana, am I glad to see you!"

Lana chuckled, the sound cascading over Helicity like cool water over cobblestones. "Same here." She interlaced her fingers and tapped the pointers against her chin. "Now then. Tell me everything about your life that I've missed."

Helicity started with her turbulent plane ride to Texas and her daily routine with Mia at the Beachside. She described meeting Trey—but because Sam was right there, she brushed over it a bit more quickly than she normally would have—while helping the stranded dolphin and how surprised she'd been when Sam and Andy showed up unannounced. She told Lana about the wild derecho that had injured both Mia and Trey—but not about finding Mia's pain medication in Andy's belongings. The fewer people who knew of her brother's situation, the better.

She finished with her story of being trapped in the lighthouse during the hurricane. Lana shook her head as if dazed. "I honestly don't know how you made it through all that, Helicity. I truly don't."

"Actually, you helped." Helicity fished out her necklace and dangled it so Lana could see the charms. "Your lightning bolt was like a talisman for me. Holding it gave me strength."

Lana looked astonished. "I thought the necklace

had been lost in the flash flood. But you've had it this whole time? Oh, Hel." Her face was wreathed in smiles. "Seeing you wearing it has done more for me than any post-coma therapy ever could."

"Well, don't get used to it being around my neck," Helicity said, "because I'm giving the necklace back the second I see you."

"Which is going to be soon." Sam leaned in to share the screen with Helicity. His closeness set off butterflies in her stomach, but she kept her expression neutral. Or she thought she did until she saw Lana's eyes flick from her to Sam and back again, as if she'd detected something between them.

Sam, luckily, seemed oblivious. "We're going to start the drive home this afternoon, assuming Helicity gets discharged from the hospital in time."

"We are? Wait, who's 'we'?" Helicity asked.

"Your mom, you, and me, in my car. Your dad and Andy will follow later." A look from Sam warned her not to ask more.

"Well, I'd better get some rest if I'm going to be ready for you two," Lana joked. She blew them both a kiss, then signed off.

Helicity handed Sam his phone, frowning. "What's going on, Sam? Why aren't Dad and Andy going home now, too?"

Sam eased onto the bed next to her, his arm resting on the pillow above her head. "Because Andy needs to stay right where he is for now," he murmured. "And your dad refused to leave him here alone. Your mom wanted to fly home, but I told her about your flight here and convinced her that we should drive back together instead." He grasped a lock of her hair and, with a smile, gave it a gentle tug. "So, I hope you're okay with spending a few days cooped up in a car with me."

There was a time not too long ago when Helicity had wanted nothing else. And now, with his fingers toying with her hair and her heart thudding in her chest, she discovered she still wanted it. "Yeah," she whispered. "I'm okay with that."

Helicity's parents arrived an hour later bearing lunch. They had been to see the facility where Andy was getting treatment, and later, Mr. Dunlap would return to the hotel near there. He drew Sam aside to consult with him about the trip back to Michigan. Helicity noted with amazement how dramatically his attitude toward the teenager had changed. In her father's eyes, it seemed, the bad boy had become the hero who had saved his son's life and tried to save his daughter's, too.

While Mr. Dunlap handled the discharge paperwork, Helicity showered and changed into clothes retrieved from the suitcase she'd stowed in Sam's car before the hurricane. In the parking lot, her father smoothed her damp hair from her forehead, a gentle gesture she remembered from when she was a small child. "Helicity, my little whirlwind who always has her head in the clouds," he murmured. "You are turning into a remarkable young woman, you know that?"

Helicity was struck speechless. She knew her father loved her but couldn't remember him ever calling her remarkable—or a young woman. She threw her arms around him, her eyes brimming with tears. "Tell Andy I love him," she whispered. "And I love you, too, Daddy." Then she climbed in the back of Sam's baby-blue sedan, and with her mother in front and Sam in the driver's seat, prepared for the journey back home. But before they pulled out of their parking space, her father stopped them.

"Almost forgot to give you this!" He handed her a package through the open window. Inside was a brand-new cell phone. "It's programmed with your same number and your contacts. And it's fully charged." He cocked an eyebrow at her, and she grinned, anticipating what he was going to say.

"Don't worry, Dad. I'll keep it charged. I promise."

And then they were off.

The trip home took two days. Helicity's mother and Sam traded off driving. They listened to podcasts, audiobooks, and music to pass the time on the long stretches of highway. Sometimes, they drove in silence so the passengers could catch a short nap. They ate at roadside restaurants—"greasy spoons," her mother called them with a laugh—and slept in chain hotels, Helicity and her mother in one room and Sam in another. They swam in the hotel pools, grateful for the chance to work the kinks out of their stiff muscles each evening and to loosen up before hitting the road again in the morning.

As they neared Michigan, Helicity struck up a text conversation with Mia.

> Almost home! Just a few more hours!

> Whoo hoo!
> I'll alert the media! LOL, JK!

> Don't you dare! LOL, NOT JK!

Mia steered the conversation to the upcoming school year, their first in high school. She texted her need to go back-to-school shopping, pondered what they should do in their last days of freedom before classes started up again, informed Helicity about who was dating whom, who had dumped whom, and similar topics of gossip. She seemed determined to keep the conversation light, and Helicity was grateful for it. But at the same time, she felt oddly distant from everything Mia was talking about. She'd go clothes shopping with Mia because she wanted to spend time with her best friend, not because she cared about showing up on the first day of high school wearing the latest trends and hottest labels. As for who was dating whom—

A thought suddenly struck her with the force of a lightning bolt.

Sam.

He was going into his senior year. They'd be at the same school. Passing through the same halls, eating in the same lunchroom, attending the same sporting events, and participating in activities. But would they be doing all those things separately? Or would they be together dating as boyfriend and girlfriend?

She remembered couples in middle school, how they'd mooned over one another only to break up a few weeks later. All she knew about high-school dating was what she'd observed Andy doing. He had taken a girl to homecoming his junior year and another to prom his senior year but never pursued anything further with either. He was too focused on football to have a serious relationship, he told them, but hoped they could remain friends. The homecoming date had understood. The girl he'd taken to the prom was much less forgiving, she recalled.

She believed Sam had feelings for her. Strong feelings, even. Strong enough to want to date her?

And do I want to date him? The thought surprised her. She really liked Sam. Had given herself shivers on more than one occasion by daydreaming she was in a romantic relationship with him. But now that those daydreams were edging closer to reality, she wondered what would happen if they actually dated.

And what it would be like if they broke up.

usk had fallen when Sam dropped Helicity and her mother at their house. It was not the house they'd rented after the tornado blasted their home to ruins, but their new place. The house had been partially constructed before the tornado. The twister had spared the structure, yet the owners had decided to find another place to live. Helicity's parents had purchased the house and finished it off that summer. Sam helped them with their luggage, gave Helicity a quick hug, and then he was gone.

Helicity's mother hefted their suitcases. "Ready to check out your new home?"

Helicity had seen phases of the renovations through video chats and photos while she was in Texas. But those images hadn't prepared her for the real thing.

The house she'd grown up in was constructed decades before she was born. The ceilings had been low, the living areas cramped, and the furniture, flooring, and fixtures scuffed and squeaky. The foyer in the new house was a wide-open space with gleaming hardwood floors. A large living room with a vaulted ceiling had a brand-new L-shaped sectional and coordinating easy chairs. An oversize television hung above a gas fireplace. The kitchen sparkled with stainless steel appliances and white cabinets. A small enclosed office and a half bathroom completed the first floor.

Helicity felt as if she'd walked into a stranger's house.

Her mother led the way upstairs to the bedrooms. "Whoa. It's so *big*!" Helicity marveled when she saw her room. She trailed her fingers over the new desk, then gave the bed—a full-size, not a twin—a test bounce.

"I went with a coastal theme," her mother said, "like the room you shared with Mia at the Beachside." Her expression clouded over. "You can change it, though, if it brings back too many . . . memories."

Helicity took in the sky-blue walls, driftwood-gray furniture, and sea-glass-green bedding, and shook her head. "Most of my memories of the Beachside are really good, Mom. So, I'm not changing anything."

Her mother smiled with relief. "The stuff you left behind in the rental house is in your closet. Andy's bedroom is on the other side of the hall bathroom."

A shadow of defeat crossed her mother's face when she mentioned Andy. She sank down beside Helicity, shoulders slumped. Helicity leaned against her. "Here's hoping he and Dad will be home really soon."

They sat that way for a few minutes. Then Mrs. Dunlap left to pick up Thai food for dinner and Helicity explored Andy's room, the bathroom, and her parents' master suite. She realized with a start that she was tiptoeing as if she were an intruder.

I'm not used to it yet, that's all, she thought. *I just need a little time to feel at home.*

She retreated downstairs to the kitchen just as her

mother returned with the food. "I'll get the plates and silverware," Helicity offered. Then she paused. "Um, where are they?"

It turned out her mother wasn't sure, either. "We put everything away just before we flew to Texas." Her brow furrowed with frustration as she yanked open drawers. "No. No. No—aha!" She brandished a pair of forks. "Now we just need plates, which are . . . here? Yes. Got it on the first try."

"New dishes?" Helicity asked. Then she made a face at her own foolishness. "Duh. Of course, we have new dishes."

"We have new *everything*," her mother said with a hint of bitterness. She held up a hand when Helicity shot her a surprised look. "Don't get me wrong, I know how lucky we are to have this house when others are still struggling to get back on their feet. It's just . . . I miss our old stuff, I guess."

"Our old stuff, yeah." Helicity waved her fork in a circle to indicate their surroundings. "Everything here is so—"

"Perfect," she and her mother said in the same breath.

"Exactly!" Helicity gestured to a piece of artwork hanging on a wall. "That flower print is pretty, but it doesn't *mean* anything to me. Not like that photo of you and Dad watching the sunset that used to hang in the hallway."

"Or that one of you as a toddler, catching snow-flakes on your tongue, and of Andy doing a muscle pose in his first football uniform," her mother chimed in.

Helicity grinned. "And we can't forget Andy's candy dish!" Her brother had crafted the misshapen clay bowl in his third-grade art class, painted it a sickly yellow-green—a color her father had dubbed "snot" when Andy was out of earshot—and presented it with great pride to their parents for Christmas. It had sat like a squashed toad on their coffee table ever since.

Her mother burst out laughing. "Oh, Lord, that hideous thing! He told me I could eat cereal out of it. I convinced him it was better for candy. *Wrapped* candy, in case that awful paint flecked off." She chuckled again.

Talking about Andy's candy dish conjured up other family memories. As they ate, she and her mother traded stories, laughing at some until tears rolled down their cheeks. By dessert, the strangeness of the new house had started to fade away.

She went to bed feeling lighter than she had in days. She draped her necklace over her bedside table lamp and brushed a fingertip on the dangling charms to make them spin. The lightning bolt and tiny glass bottle winked and flashed in the soft light. She watched them until they stopped moving, then turned off the lamp and fell asleep within minutes.

She slept soundly at first. Then darkness crept into her dreams, and a nightmare like one she'd had in Texas returned.

She was adrift in a boat on a foggy sea, desperately trying to save Andy from a malevolent force dragging him below the inky surface. A swirling vortex opened beneath him. Family pictures and belongings, his clay pot—everything was sucked below. "Don't lose me, too!" Andy cried as he slipped from her grasp.

The whirlpool closed over his head. She thrashed at the still water, sobbing. Suddenly, the surface erupted and Andy shot out. But it wasn't the real Andy. It was an imposter with hollowed-out eye sockets and a thick chain around his neck. The chain disappeared into the water. Far below, a figure wearing a shark-tooth necklace yanked the other end, making Not-Andy jerk forward. The figure grinned.

He's mine now.

Helicity bolted upright, the figure's taunt echoing in her head. Heart hammering, she threw back the covers, raced down the hall to her parents' bedroom, and crawled into the king-size bed.

"Helicity? Helicity, what's wrong?"

Helicity trembled as she replayed the nightmare for her mother. "What if we can't get our Andy back, Mom? What if we lost him to—to—" She couldn't finish.

Her mother gripped her in a tight embrace and stroked her hair. "Andy is strong, Hel. With lots of support, ours and people trained to guide him, I believe he'll get through this. But before he can come back to us, he has to find himself first. That's something only he can do. All you and I and Dad can do is be here for him when he gets home."

Helicity nodded against her shoulder. They lay quietly, each lost in her own thoughts. In time, her mother's breathing turned slow and even, signaling she'd fallen asleep. Helicity slipped from her embrace and returned to her own room. She stared out her window at the moon until her eyelids finally closed and she, too, slept.

CHAPTER EIGHT

T he next morning, Helicity's doctor gave her a thorough examination and asked her a clip- boardful of questions. She must have been satisfied with the results for she told Helicity she could resume her normal activities. "Not all at once and nothing too strenuous," she warned.

From the doctor's office, Helicity and her mother went to the nearby community college where Mrs. Dunlap worked. Sam met Helicity there and, together, they drove to Lana's house. Helicity was so excited to see her mentor that she couldn't sit still.

"You're like a little kid going to meet Santa Claus," Sam said with a sideways grin.

"Lana's way better than Santa," Helicity scoffed.

Sam considered that for a moment, then said, "Yeah, she is."

As they approached Lana's street, Helicity's phone buzzed. Her forehead puckered in a frown when she read Mia's text.

"Problem?" Sam queried.

"Mia and I were going to hang out this afternoon. Now she says she can't. And I really needed to see her."

Sam nodded slowly. "To tell her about Andy."

Helicity swallowed hard. "Yeah."

Mia was her best friend. Yet she'd kept the truth about her brother from her. Before the hurricane, the information was still so new, so raw, that she hadn't even processed it herself. Plus, Mia had been so anxious about the pending hurricane, Helicity refused to add to her stress. Afterward, when Mia had asked why Andy and her father weren't coming back to Michigan with them, she'd given a vague answer about there not being enough room in Sam's car, and then quickly changed the subject. Explaining the real situation over the phone or through texts just didn't seem right.

She'd planned to tell Mia everything that afternoon. But now it would have to wait.

They pulled into Lana's driveway a minute later. Helicity flew up the bungalow's front steps, knocked on the door, and eagerly peered through the glass sidelights. She'd been expecting Lana to answer, but to her surprise and delight, an older man with tight gray curls and a slight paunch opened the door.

"Ray! I didn't know you were here!"

Ray was Lana's longtime storm-chasing partner and friend. A techno whiz with a truck full of specialized equipment for tracking and recording weather events, he knew more about the atmosphere than anyone Helicity had ever met—except Lana, that is. He acted gruff, but after spending time on the road with him earlier that summer, she knew he had a soft side, too.

The twinkle in his eye gave away his pleasure at seeing them. *Both* of them, Helicity noted with relief. Ray and Sam had built a good relationship during their summer storm-chasing excursion. But

Sam's reckless actions had been partly to blame for Lana nearly losing her life in the flash flood. Helicity had played a big part in that disaster, too, but she'd made her peace with Ray before leaving for Texas. Now she saw that Sam and Ray had patched things up as well.

"Hey, old-timer." Sam clasped Ray's hand and gave him an impish grin.

"Good to see you, troublemaker." Ray pulled him into a one-armed embrace, then swept Helicity into the hug, too. "Even better to see *you*."

"Is that Helicity?" a voice called from inside.

Helicity's heart leaped. "Lana!" She started to push past Ray.

He stopped her with a gentle hand on her shoulder. Concern deepened the lines of his craggy face. "Before you go in, I want to prepare you."

"For what?" Sam asked.

"For Lana." Ray blew out a deep breath. "She's only been out of the coma for a week, remember. So far, her recovery has been going well. But she's a far cry from her old self. She's lost a lot of weight and muscle tone. She's shaky on her feet and sometimes her attention wanders. Her memory has gaps. Rest is the best thing for her, rest and absolutely no stress, which is why she's taking a leave of absence from teaching this year. And why you have to keep your visit short and your conversation light. Okay?"

He stepped aside. Helicity hurried into the living room with Sam right behind her.

Lana reclined on a sofa, feet propped on an ottoman. During their video chat two days earlier, she'd looked a little worn down. In person, she looked exhausted. The skin beneath her eyes was pouched and wrinkled like deflated balloons, and her cheekbones stood out in sharp angles. Her body, once so full of boundless energy, seemed permanently molded to the cushions. She raised a hand in greeting, then let it fall back with a soft thud as if the effort of holding it up was too much for her. Even her smile looked tired.

"Hey." The word escaped Lana's lips in a whisper.

"Hey," Helicity responded. She sank down on the sofa and drew Lana into a gentle hug. The bony feel of Lana's protruding shoulder blades made her want to weep. "Hey, I have something for you, remember?"

A shadow of confusion crossed Lana's face, and Helicity cursed herself for forgetting Ray's warning about her memory. "It's your necklace. I've been keeping it safe for you."

She removed the chain and dangled it where Lana could see the charms. Lana blinked rapidly. Then her focus seemed to sharpen, and she smiled. "My necklace. I thought I lost it."

"No, it's been with me. But now it's time for me to give it back."

But when Helicity tried to loop the necklace over Lana's head, Lana stopped her. "Please keep it. It makes me happy to know you're wearing the lightning bolt." With a slight grunt of effort, she reached up and captured the tiny bottle. "Besides, I like the way this dolphin looks next to it. So, please, keep them together. For me."

"For you?" Helicity slowly hung the necklace back around her own neck. "Anything."

Sudden tears made it impossible for her to say more. But when she searched Lana's face, she realized there was nothing more she needed to say. Lana might not be 100 percent now. But like the sun hiding behind a cloud, Helicity believed the old Lana, the one who shared her passion for weather and cared for her like a daughter, was still there. And just as the sun always emerged eventually, so, too, would Lana, as bright and glowing as ever.

Not long afterward, Ray caught Helicity's eye and gave a subtle nod. It was time to go.

On the car ride home, Helicity stared out the window, hand clasped around the necklace charms.

"I didn't know."

She started at the sound of Sam's voice. "Didn't know what?"

"How bad off she is. How much she's suffered. Because"—his Adam's apple bobbed with his hard swallow—"because of me."

"Sam. Don't."

"It could have been you, you know." He gripped the steering wheel tighter. "When I think of the danger I put you in, chasing after that storm. Well, never again." He looked over at her. "You have my word on that."

Helicity held his gaze, unsure what he was promising. To never chase a storm again? Or to never put her in danger? And how could he possibly promise either? As she tried to think of something to say, a flash of color caught the corner of her eye.

"Sam! Red light!"

Sam hit the brakes seconds before careering through an intersection. As the car jerked to a stop, he flung his arm across her chest, pressing her back against her seat. "Fifteen! Are you okay?"

Her heart was racing, but he sounded panicked, so she made light of it. "I'm totally fine. Really." She glanced down at his arm and grinned. "My mom does the same move."

He blinked, then dropped his arm. "Yeah, well, she just wants to protect you, too."

They both turned their attention back to the road. A flock of girls in matching team tank tops and spandex running shorts jogged in front of the car.

"Who are they, some kind of running group?" Helicity wondered.

"High-school girls' cross-country team. Preseason practice," Sam supplied.

Helicity made a face. "Ugh, who would ever run unless they had to? Not me, that's for—"

She broke off suddenly and stared in disbelief at one of the runners. Small in stature, the girl had been hidden by the others before. "That's Mia!"

"**M**ia? Seriously?" Sam watched the runners pass with interest. "Since when is
she a runner?"

"Since never!" *And stop staring at those girls,* she
wanted to add.

The teammates funneled through a gate to a field,
circled up, and started their cooldown exercises. "Pull
into the parking lot, Sam," Helicity urged. She waited
impatiently until the girls were done, then got out and
hurried to the field. Excitement at reuniting with her

best friend mingled with confusion that Mia hadn't said anything about running with the cross-country team.

There's a lot you haven't told her either, a little voice inside her reminded her.

As Helicity searched for Mia in the throng, an older girl with long, muscular legs and a high ponytail of shiny brown hair separated from the group and approached her. "I know you. You're Andy Dunlap's little sister, Felicity. No, wait, that's not it." She snapped her fingers. "It's *Hel*icity! Right?"

"Right." Helicity recognized the girl as Andy's prom date, Kate Marshall. "Hi, Kate. How are you?"

"Good, good." Kate released her ponytail and threaded her fingers through her silky hair. "So, how's your brother doing? I heard about his accident. Sure hope he's okay."

She sounded concerned, but Helicity wasn't fooled. After prom, Kate had shown up at the house, furious that Andy wanted to be "just friends." She accused him of leading her on, of using her just so he didn't have to go to prom without a date, of humiliating her by dumping her immediately afterward. Andy had appeared cowed, but after Kate stormed off, his expression changed to relief. When Helicity had asked him why he didn't want to date Kate, he'd scratched his head and replied, "Honestly? She got this look in her eye sometimes, like she was sizing me up, looking for weaknesses. I get enough of that on the football field. Don't need it off the field, too."

That conversation came back to Helicity now as Kate zeroed in on her like a cat eyeballing a mouse. "Andy's fine," she answered guardedly. "I'm actually here to see a friend of mine, so if you'll excuse me . . ."

Kate went on as if she hadn't spoken. "Where is your brother, anyway? After that tornado, it was like he fell off the face of the earth. What's he been up to this summer?"

Helicity froze. She realized she should have anticipated questions like this. After all, Andy had been the talk of the town last year, first for leading the football team to the state championship and then for getting a huge athletic scholarship to Michigan State. But what kind of answer could she possibly give about what he was doing now—or planning to do in the future, for that matter?

As she fumbled for a reply, Kate's eyes gleamed as if she'd picked up on Helicity's discomfort and took pleasure in it. "He—he was around," Helicity finally stammered. "Busy with physical therapy, mostly. And he's taking a gap year instead of going straight to college." It wasn't a total lie; Andy had been doing PT before he took off with Sam for Texas, and he wasn't heading to Michigan State—or any college, most likely—that year. She didn't like telling a half-truth, but there was no chance she'd tell Kate anything more.

Kate studied her a moment longer, then shrugged. "A gap year, huh? That's cool. I mean, what else was he going to do now that his football career is over?"

The casual way she referred to Andy's loss made Helicity seethe. But she held her tongue, afraid she might say something she'd later regret.

"*Helicity!* Ohmygod-ohmygod-ohmygod!"

Someone tackled her from behind. Helicity spun and wrapped her arms around her assailant. "Mia!"

"This is your friend?"

At Kate's question, Helicity and Mia broke apart. Mia was grinning like an idiot, tears in her eyes.

"Helicity is my *best* friend," she told Kate, "and for a few days, I thought I lost her."

Kate arched an eyebrow. "Lost her?"

Something in her tone put Helicity on guard again. She wanted to warn Mia to keep quiet about Texas, but she couldn't think of a way of doing so without heightening Kate's interest even more.

"You know that hurricane in the Gulf of Mexico?" Mia said. "Helicity was stuck in a lighthouse on Bolivar Peninsula during the whole thing! And she not only survived, she was a hero. Saved a little girl's dog."

Helicity started. She hadn't mentioned Scout in their texts or phone calls. It would have sounded like she was bragging, she thought. "Wait, how did you hear about that?"

"Trey sent me a link to the television clip of the girl's dad giving you a shout-out."

"Your act of heroism was mentioned on TV? Wow." Kate widened her eyes as if she was impressed. "Andy must be so proud of you."

Kate's laser-like focus on Andy unnerved Helicity. She started to redirect the conversation to another subject, but Mia spoke before she could. "Andy was almost caught in the hurricane, too, but he made it out before the storm hit."

"Is that right? Huh." Kate's gaze slid to Helicity. "I thought he was here in Michigan all summer, doing PT."

Helicity willed herself not to look away. "Not *all* summer," she amended defensively.

"And he sure wasn't doing PT in Texas," Mia added with a laugh. "Unless that deadbeat Johnny was his therapist, which I highly doubt! Man, that guy was creepy, wasn't he, Hel? With that shark-tooth necklace he always wore? *Ugh*." She shuddered with disgust.

Kate eyed Helicity for a moment longer, then smiled. "Well, it's good to see you, Helicity. Tell Andy hey for me. Mia, see you at my house." She picked up her gear and walked off toward the parking lot.

Mia flung her arms around Helicity again. "It's so good to see you!"

"You, too." Helicity pulled back. "Is that why you can't hang out with me? Because you're going to Kate's house?"

Mia nodded. "She's the cross-country team captain.

She's hosting a lunch and team-building thing today. You're not mad that I had to cancel our plans, are you?"

"Mad? No. Curious? Heck, yes!" Helicity plucked at Mia's team tank top. "When did this whole running thing happen? And why?"

Mia took a long drink from her water bottle before answering. "Actually, it's because of you."

Helicity blinked. "Uh, come again?"

"When you went missing during the hurricane, I—I sort of lost it. I spent two days yelling at the phone to ring with news, calling your parents every hour for updates, clicking through websites for information about survivors, and . . . well, crying, basically."

"Oh, Mia." A wave of anguish for her friend's stress washed over Helicity.

"When I finally heard you'd been found . . ." Mia smiled tremulously. "Hel, I thought I was going to burst I was so relieved. Instead, I ran. Don't ask me why. It just felt *right*." She gave a little laugh. "You know those dirt roads and fields that go from my house to the hill? You know, the one where you saw the tornado forming?"

Helicity nodded. The memory of that day always

hovered in the back of her mind—and of another, later day, when she'd stood atop the same hill and made a vow to be a survivor, not a victim. A vow she'd somehow kept despite the disasters she'd been swept up in.

"That's where I ran. To the top of the hill and back. Someone on the team saw me and invited me to join them at practice the next morning. That was three days and three practices ago." Mia paused. "Running through the woods and fields and up and down hills—I know it seems crazy, Hel, but I really like it. And I think I might be good at it, too," she added shyly. "I overheard one of the seniors say I'm the best freshman on the team."

A warm glow settled over Helicity at Mia's happiness. "That's awesome. Seriously, I'm psyched for you, even though we'll have even less time to hang out. I mean, if your practices and games—"

"*Meets.* Competitions are called meets."

"Right. If you're as busy with cross-country as Andy was with football, then we won't see each other until after Thanksgiving!" She meant it as a joke but there was some truth to it. High-school sports took up a huge chunk of an athlete's time. She wouldn't see Mia much during school hours, either. Thanks to tutoring from Sam earlier in the summer, Helicity had bumped up to higher-level courses than Mia, who had a learning disability, was able to take. She looked forward to the new academic challenges, but it meant she and Mia would be in different classes for the first time ever.

One of the older girls called to Mia. "Hey, frosh! I've got room for one more in my car. You want in?"

Mia shouldered her gear and looked at Helicity. "You sure you don't mind me going?"

"Of course not. But listen, can you sleep over tonight? I really want to catch up."

Mia agreed, then hurried off to join her teammates. Helicity started back to Sam's car. As she pulled open the door, another car drove past her. Kate was behind the wheel. She was wearing mirrored aviator sunglasses that hid her eyes. Yet Helicity had an uneasy feeling those eyes were studying her.

Like Kate was looking for a weakness.

CHAPTER TEN

"**A**ndy is an addict. *Andy.* Your brother."

Mia stared at Helicity, her jaw slack with shock. She had arrived after dinner with her pajamas and pillow. Helicity gave her a quick tour of the new house and then hustled her upstairs to her bedroom, sat her down, and told her about Andy.

Mia flopped back onto the bed. "The whole time he was in Texas—"

"And before that," Helicity interjected. "Ever since the tornado. It's why he left Michigan in the first place, I think. To get away from my parents so they wouldn't find out."

She could see Mia's mind working to put the pieces together. "So, Johnny . . ."

"A creepy deadbeat, like you told Kate. And Andy's dealer." Helicity spat out the last words like a mouthful of spoiled milk.

"The night we were robbed, when the burglar cleaned out Suze's wallet and our tip jar . . . that was *Andy*?"

"Yeah." Helicity picked at a loose thread on her T-shirt. "He took your pills, too."

"The painkillers the hospital gave me." Mia's hand stole to her upper back, where the boom of a sailboat had struck her during the wild winds of the derecho.

Helicity nodded. "I found the bottle in his duffel. I might never have known what was going on with him otherwise." She drew her knees to her chest and hugged them tightly. "I should have figured it out sooner. It was all right in front of me. The way he was acting, the way he looked, God, even the way he *smelled*." She twisted a lock of her hair savagely around her fingers. "I asked him more than once if something was wrong, but he pushed me away. And I let him when I should have pushed back. But I didn't, not until that pill bottle was in my hand." She dropped her hair and stared at her palm. Instead of the thick bandage covering her wound, she saw the bottle there, glowing orange in the headlights of Sam's car. Felt Andy's despair, his helpless, desperate rage, when she emptied the pills into her palm and hurled them into the Gulf of Mexico.

Mia sat up and touched Helicity's arm. "Hey, none of us suspected what was going on, Hel. Not your parents, not Suze, not Sam, and certainly not me. So we all share the blame."

They stayed that way for a long moment. Then Mia lay back down and gave Helicity the side-eye. "There's something you're not sharing, though, isn't there?"

Helicity blinked. "What? No, I—"

"You and Trey kissed. He texted me about it."

"Oh." Helicity flushed to her roots. "That."

"Yeah. *That.* Wasn't a love connection, huh?" When Helicity lifted a shoulder, Mia shook her head. "Too bad. Trey's a great guy."

"Absolutely."

"And he was greatly bummed out when he realized you weren't feeling it."

Helicity lowered her gaze. She liked Trey, she really did . . . just not in the way he wanted her to. "I'm sorry if I hurt him. I didn't mean to. But even if I wanted something more, he lives in Texas. It's not like we could date or anything."

"Mmm, true. Unlike the possibility of dating, say, Sam?" Mia held up a hand when Helicity protested. "Come on, Hel. It's obvious you're into him. But let's have a little reality check, hmm? If he hasn't made a move by now, he's not going to."

Helicity squirmed. "Actually, he did."

"*What?*" Mia shot bolt upright.

"One kiss, that's it!"

"One *great* kiss, judging by the look on your face."

Helicity's hands flew to her flaming cheeks, making Mia laugh.

"Busted! So, what happened next?"

Helicity rolled her eyes. "You mean besides me getting trapped in a lighthouse during a hurricane, Sam rescuing my brother, and then the trip back here with my mother as chaperone? Not a whole lot of opportunity for anything *next*, Mia."

That wasn't exactly true, though, she realized. Her flush returned when she recalled how tender Sam had been in the hospital.

"Man, you've got the worst poker face ever!" Mia teased. "Come on. Give."

"It's nothing," Helicity evaded. "He was nice to me in the hospital. That's all."

Just then, her phone rang. She snatched it up, grateful to avoid further probing questions about Sam—then groaned inwardly when his name and number blazed on the tiny screen. Mia saw it, too. With an exaggerated wink, she got up and headed to the hallway, saying, "I'll go check out your ice cream supply, give you two some alone time."

Helicity threw a pillow after her, then answered the call.

"Hey, Fifteen," Sam said, "sorry to interrupt your time with Mia, but I wanted to give you a heads-up about a message I just got from Kate Marshall."

"Kate?" Helicity's heart skipped a beat. "You know her?"

"Well, sure I *know* her. We both grew up here. But it's not like we hang out. No clue how she got my contact info."

Mia, Helicity thought with a twinge of panic. Kate could have asked her for Sam's number that afternoon. Mia would have given it to her. No reason not to; after all, Mia didn't know about Andy until ten minutes ago, wouldn't have known to keep quiet about anything remotely connected to him. *What else might she have told Kate?*

"What did she want?" she asked.

"She asked how I know you."

Like she was sizing me up, looking for weaknesses. Andy's impression of Kate raced through Helicity's mind again. "What did you tell her?"

"Nothing yet. I wanted to check in with you first. Any clue why she wants to know about us?"

Us. A thrill sizzled up Helicity's spine at the word. She quashed the feeling with a mental shake of her head and told him about her earlier encounter with the cross-country captain. "She suspects I'm hiding something about Andy, I'm sure of it."

"And she thinks we're close, and that I know what

that something is." Sam snorted. "Well, she can forget getting anything out of me. When we hang up, I'll delete her text and block her number so she can't contact me again."

Helicity thought for a moment. "No, don't. That'll just make her more suspicious. Instead, tell her . . ." Helicity cast her gaze around the room, looking for inspiration. She spotted an old notebook of math assignments in her closet. "Tell her you tutored me at the beginning of summer. If she asks why I was in your car today, say we were visiting a sick friend together."

"Got it." Sam's voice turned amused. "You know, for a dog-saving hero, you're pretty good at lying."

"I'm not a hero, and they're not lies!" Helicity protested. "Just not the whole story." Her conscience poked at her for once again hiding behind a shield of half-truths. She ignored it. Then something else occurred to her. "To convince her we're not, you know, *close* . . . maybe we shouldn't spend so much time together. Or—or any. Just in case."

Sam was silent. "Yeah, that's probably a good idea," he finally agreed. "Makes me feel sorry for you and Mia, though."

"Why?"

"Because I was going to offer you rides to school. Now you'll have to take the bus."

She laughed. "I'll manage."

"You always do. And don't worry, Fifteen. Andy's secret is safe with me."

"I know."

But as she hung up, Helicity wondered if her brother's secret was safe with anyone. Kate didn't strike her as someone who gave up easily. More like a bloodhound that's caught the scent, she thought as she went downstairs to find Mia, and won't quit until it's cornered its prey.

CHAPTER ELEVEN

"Tell me again why we're taking the bus instead of getting a ride with Sam?" Mia groused two days later.

"Because we're not on his way, our parents paid for our passes, and no senior boy wants to show up on the first day of school with two freshmen girls in his car." Helicity had decided against telling Mia the real reason. Cross-country was too important to Mia, and she didn't want her to be on edge around the team's captain. Besides, now that Mia knew about Andy,

Helicity trusted she wouldn't say a word about him to Kate or anyone else.

The girls parted when they entered the school. It felt strange to navigate the hallways without Mia by her side, and even stranger to look away when she and Sam locked eyes across the lunchroom. But her teachers, many of whom asked after Andy, were nice. She knew most of her classmates, and the coursework seemed manageable. So, when her father quizzed her over the phone that evening, she was able to give high school a thumbs-up.

Mr. Dunlap called them most nights to update them on Andy's progress. His visits to the rehabilitation center were brief, but what he saw in his son made him cautiously optimistic. "He's not there yet, but he's one step closer than he was yesterday," he said at the end of each call.

After one more day of school, the students were off for the long Labor Day weekend. Helicity found herself with nothing to do and no one to do it with. Mia was at her grandmother's house, Sam was camping with his father, and her mother was at her office catching up on work. At first, Helicity enjoyed the lazy pace. But by Monday morning, she was going crazy from boredom. So, when Ray called asking for help packing up Lana's college office, Helicity jumped at the chance.

She arrived on campus before Ray. Stale air enveloped her when she pushed open Lana's door. She clicked on a tabletop fan that sent dust motes whirling through a beam of morning sunlight. Her gaze passed over a withered potted plant and a yellowed newspaper clipping of a younger Lana, then paused at the wall of weather-themed movie posters—*Twister, The Wizard of Oz, Sharknado*—and framed photographs of cloud formations, sunsets, and storms.

Her own photo of the Memorial Day tornado, taken moments before the heavy dark clouds began to spiral into a funnel, hung among the others. She brushed her fingertips across the dusty glass.

Everything that happened this summer started with this storm, she thought. *If I hadn't been on the hill that day, Andy wouldn't have been in the car accident. If I hadn't taken this picture, I wouldn't have met Lana or Sam or—*

"A dollar for your thoughts."

Helicity spun around. Ray stood in the doorway with an armload of plastic bins and a tote bag of cleaning supplies.

"A dollar?" Helicity said, taking the tote from him. "I thought it was a penny."

"Nah. Your thoughts are worth more than that." Ray dumped the bins on the floor. "Although I'll bet I can guess what you were thinking. But don't you worry, Hel—Lana's a fighter. She'll be back eventually." He picked up the dead plant and made a face. "This, on the other hand, is beyond hope."

Ray took charge of Lana's files, leaving Helicity to pack up her personal belongings. Despite Ray's assurances that Lana would return, the packing had an air of finality that depressed her.

Ray's throaty chuckle pulled her out of her melancholy. "Take a look at these." He handed her a folder labeled BIZARRE! Inside were pages of articles and photographs of strange weather phenomena. A vast ice disk that had formed on a river in Maine. A skinny, ground-to-sky coil of fire—dubbed a "firenado"—that had spun up in England. Snow in Eastern Europe that had turned shades of orange and yellow from sand carried on the wind from the Sahara Desert. Helicity had read about many of the events herself. She'd been fascinated by each and even more intrigued by the unique conditions—rapid changes in water temperature and river currents, extreme heat combined with whirling wind, windstorms powerful enough to send sand into the atmosphere—that had caused them.

"Lana always led off her first class of the semester with these kinds of stories. Her students loved them." Ray paused. "And her."

Helicity looked up from a startling image of a waterspout so enormous it dwarfed nearby buildings. "I hope I can take her classes someday."

Ray smiled. "Honey, you already know more about the weather than most of her students combined. But yeah. I hope you can, too." He nodded toward the folder. "Take that if you want. Your tornado photo, too."

"Thanks, Ray."

Ray dropped her at home when they were finished. Up in her room, she propped the tornado photo on her desk, then paged through the BIZARRE! folder again. A list of words she hadn't seen earlier fell out.

Swullocking, blind smuir, blenky: she wrinkled her nose with confusion. Then she came to a term she recognized: *haboob*, an Arabic word for a violent sandstorm. She remembered giggling the first time she'd heard it. But there was nothing funny about the disastrous effects such storms had on human health, the environment, and communities—effects made all the worse by the unpredictable nature of haboobs.

She ran down the list again, now knowing the words were bizarre weather terms. She'd just discovered that *smullocking* was an old-fashioned word for hot, humid conditions when she heard her mother come home.

"Helicity? You up there?"

Helicity tucked the list back in the folder and hurried down to the kitchen. Her mother was pulling out bread and cheese for grilled cheese sandwiches. "So," Mrs. Dunlap said, "I have the afternoon free. Anything special you'd like to do?"

Helicity brightened. "Actually, there is."

Since returning to Michigan, she had been longing to ride her horse, Raven. Her mother had insisted she wait a week per the doctor's orders to avoid any strenuous activity. But now the week was up. So after lunch,

Mrs. Dunlap dropped her at the stables where Raven had been boarded since the tornado. "I'll be back in three hours," she called before driving off.

In the barn, Raven stuck his head over the stall door and nickered a greeting. She could tell Raven was so happy to see her by that gleam in his eye. Or maybe that was her over-reading the situation, but whatever the case, Raven felt like one of the only parts of her old life that kept her grounded and feeling connected. Helicity moved in close, ran her hand over the velvety fur of his neck, and breathed in the familiar earthy smell of hay and manure and horse sweat. "Come on, boy. Let's get out of here."

As they galloped across the open field, Helicity lost herself in the freedom that came with riding Raven. The thunder of his hoofbeats, the wind in her hair, and the flex and bunch of his muscles—she wanted to shout with joy. She gave Raven his head, knowing where he would go. Sure enough, he raced to her favorite hill, slowing only when the gentle incline steepened and narrowed. Around one bend they passed a jagged stump, all that remained of the shattered tree that had nearly crushed them during the tornado.

At the summit, Helicity surveyed the land below from Raven's back. Trees, farm fields, and roadways spread out like a museum diorama. Her heart filled with pride when she saw her town. Huge sections had been ravaged by the tornado, but the people refused to let their community die. The faraway streets bustled with activity as people rebuilt their homes, their businesses, their lives.

Much farther away, other people were just beginning the same process on the Bolivar Peninsula. Her father had volunteered to help, she and her mother learned the night before. "I'm going nuts with nothing to do here but wait to see Andy, so I reached out to Mia's aunt Suze, who put me in touch with some people." His experience with heavy-duty construction equipment was welcomed with open arms, and both Helicity and her mother could tell he was pleased to be of use. His good mood had a ripple effect, making them both feel more relaxed. And more hopeful.

Helicity let those same feelings wash through her as she climbed off Raven and onto a sun-warmed boulder. Only the gentle sound of Raven cropping grass broke the silence as she watched a single white cloud

drift across the brilliant blue sky. For the first time since her return to Michigan, she felt completely at peace.

A blaring ring from her phone shattered the calm. And when she answered, her peace fled.

"**H**el!" Mia's anxiety traveled through the phone and gripped Helicity by the throat. "I need you to come to my house. *Now.*"

"Mia, what's wrong?"

"Everything. Can you get here?"

Helicity glanced at Raven. "Yes."

"Hurry."

Mia disconnected. Helicity stared at the blank screen, then shoved the phone in her pocket and dashed to Raven's side. The horse gave a surprised whinny when she snatched up the reins and swung onto his back. With an insistent nudge of her boots, she urged him down the hillside path. Memories of her panicked ride down this same hill before the tornado assaulted her mind. She could almost feel the pea-size hail pummeling her body.

There was no hail this time, just adrenaline-stoked fear that twisted her stomach in knots as she galloped across the fields and over the dirt roads that led to Mia's house.

Mia was outside, pacing on her front stoop, eyes darting back and forth as she read something on her phone. She rushed over when Helicity dismounted. Her cheeks were streaked with tears.

"Oh, Hel. Social media is blowing up."

Helicity stared at her uncomprehendingly.

"Andy," Mia whispered. "It's all about Andy." Her face crumpled. "And it's all my fault."

Helicity's heart skipped a beat. She grabbed Mia's hand and pulled her inside. "Show me."

Mia's house was one of the few that the tornado had spared. It was as familiar to Helicity as her old home had once been, and she'd always felt comfortable within its walls. But as she took a seat at the well-worn kitchen table, her only emotion was pure dread.

Mia slumped beside her. With trembling hands, she pulled up a conversation thread on her phone. Horrible, mean-spirited comments about Andy flooded the screen.

> Did you hear about our local sports hero? Not so heroic after all! druggie

> Tsk-tsk-tsk. How the mighty have fallen.

> I played on the team with Dunlap last year. He ratted me out when he caught me drinking a beer. Hypocrite! #loser.

Helicity recognized some of the names as classmates, hers and Andy's. Their eagerness to mock her brother, to drag his reputation through the mud, made her insides churn. "How?" she asked helplessly. "I don't understand."

"Johnny. And—and Kate."

Mia scrolled to the start of the conversation. The writer, who went by the name Katydid, had dropped a teaser: *Looks like Andy Dunlap's got a new friend . . . and maybe a new habit.* The post included two attachments. Mia hovered her thumb over the first and shot Helicity a questioning look.

"Open it," Helicity said through gritted teeth.

A photo taken on a beach at dusk popped up. She recognized the picture immediately. It was taken at the seaside party Trey and Mia had thrown for her fourteenth birthday. Confetti dotted the white tablecloth covering a picnic table. The metallic pieces were too small to see clearly, but Helicity knew they were silver-blue and shaped like dolphins. She had one of the pieces in the tiny bottle on her necklace.

Three people—her, Andy, and Johnny—sat at the picnic table. Andy and Johnny were laughing uproariously. Helicity was leaning away from them. She was smiling, but her smile was forced, the skin around her eyes tight.

Andy's erratic behavior that night had confused her. His thoughtless gift, a hastily scrawled "coupon" for a dinner out with her brother, had hurt her feelings. Even now, weeks later and knowing what she knew about him, she had to swallow back her pain.

"I posted this pic on my account right after I took it," Mia said. "Last week, before I knew about Andy, Kate asked to follow me. Everyone on the cross-country team is connected to everyone else, not just on this site but on lots of others, so I figured I better be, too. I didn't know she'd copied the photo to her account until now because the Wi-Fi at my grand-mother's house is basically nonexistent. And then there's this."

She zoomed in on Johnny and looked at Helicity again.

For a second, Helicity didn't understand. Then realization dawned on her. "His shark-tooth neck-lace." She stared at the leather cord around Johnny's neck. Despite the photo's dark quality, the triangular teeth were easy to identify. "You mentioned it to Kate that day at practice. And Johnny's name, too. But I still don't get how she or anyone else made the jump from this photo to Andy being a—a drug addict."

"Because somehow—facial recognition, trolling Bolivar websites, who knows—Kate found this." Mia clicked on the second attachment. A news article popped up. POLICE NAB SUSPECT BEHIND RASH OF

BOLIVAR BURGLARIES, the headline read. Just below was a photo of Johnny in handcuffs between two burly police officers. His head was bowed and his scraggly hair obscured his face, but his shark-tooth necklace was clearly visible. The article detailed his arrest the morning of the hurricane, stating that police had acted on an anonymous tip. Besides burglary, he was charged with possession of illegal drugs with the intent to sell. The article noted he was under the influence of opioids at the time of his arrest.

"Hold on." Helicity frowned. "There isn't anything in here about Andy, just Johnny. So where does Kate get off saying Andy was using drugs, too? And why are people reacting as if it's true when they don't have any facts to back it up? It makes no sense!"

Helicity knew she sounded naïve the moment the words left her mouth. People didn't care if they had proof, not when they had gossip and innuendo. "But . . . it's Andy! People here love him!" She raked her hands through her hair in frustration.

Mia grimaced. "Not as much as they love to see someone fail. Especially if that someone was on top or famous. Or if they feel they've been wronged. Andy broke up with Kate right after prom, right? So yeah. She feels wronged."

Helicity bit her lip. "How many people will see these posts?"

"Too many. Kate has a lot of followers. But she's going to have one less."

"What do you mean?" Helicity asked.

"I'm going to unfollow her. And tomorrow, I'm dropping out of cross-country."

Helicity was touched by Mia's loyalty. But Mia would be the one who'd suffer if she quit, not Kate. "Don't drop out, Mia. Not if you love running as much as I think you do. And stay connected, too. We need to know if she says anything more about Andy."

Helicity's phone buzzed with a text then. "Shoot, it's my mom. She's waiting for me at the stables. I gotta go." She captured Raven's reins and swung up onto his back. "I'll call you later. We'll figure out a way to shut this down before it gets out of control. In the meantime, stop blaming yourself. You didn't do anything wrong."

She wheeled around and pointed Raven toward the stables. As she rode, she debated telling her mother

what had happened. Mrs. Dunlap was on at least one social media site—almost impossible not to be in this day and age—but in her words, the platform was "a huge time suck," so she rarely logged on and refused to get notifications. There was little chance she was connected to any of Kate's followers or Kate herself, so the risk of her seeing the posts about Andy were minimal.

But if I tell her, she'll insist on seeing the posts, she thought as she and Raven trotted up the farm driveway. She could show them to herself. The accounts she'd created shortly after her birthday were linked with Mia's, so she could pull up the comment thread on her own phone. But what would reading those comments about her son do to her mother? The content was so ugly, so vengeful and hurtful and—

And true.

That reality hit her like a body blow. A lot of what people were accusing Andy of was grossly exaggerated. But drill down through it all, and you hit the truth: Andy was an addict.

And how can I fight back against the truth?

Helicity's mind was whirling so fast she almost rode right past her mother.

"Helicity!"

Helicity reined Raven to a stop and dismounted. Her mother hurried to her side. Only then did Helicity see her red-rimmed eyes, her heaving shoulders, her tear-stained face. Only then did she see the phone in her hand.

"Oh, Helicity." Mrs. Dunlap could barely get the words out. She thrust the phone into Helicity's hand. "It's Dad. About Andy."

CHAPTER THIRTEEN

*T*hey know.

Helicity's heart broke for her parents' pain—until she realized her mother's tears were joyful, not anguished. Bewildered, she raised the phone to her ear. "Dad? Everything okay?"

"Everything's wonderful!" he boomed. Helicity could hear the grin in his voice. "I was just telling Mom that Andy agreed to return to therapy."

"Return to therapy?" Helicity shot her mother a look of confusion. "I don't understand. Did he leave the treatment facility or something?"

Mr. Dunlap chuckled. "No, no, sorry, bad choice of words! He's still there, working with his counselors. I meant *physical* therapy. He says he's ready to work to regain full use of his arm. He wants to get back on the field, Hel. Back to football." His voice broke suddenly. "And he's coming back to *us*, too. If all goes well, we can head home as soon as next week!"

Helicity's emotions roller-coastered from the depths of despair to the heights of happiness in a split second. Andy—*her* Andy, *their* Andy—was fighting his way back to them. But as she handed the phone to her mother, the roller coaster topped the hill and shot back down.

He's making his way back to us. But what will be waiting for him when he gets here?

She got the answer at school the next day. Hallways, classrooms, even the girls' restroom—wherever she went, people elbowed one another and exchanged knowing glances when she walked by. They whispered and giggled behind their hands, quieted when she drew near, and whispered again when she moved past. Classmates who had been friendly to her just days before now pretended she didn't exist. She even caught a teacher narrowing his eyes suspiciously at her.

By afternoon, her jaw ached from clenching her teeth. She dragged her feet on the way to the bus, wishing that Mia was riding home with her instead of going to cross-country practice.

"Hey, Fifteen!" Sam caught up to her by the school doors. He'd returned from his camping trip the evening before and had listened, outraged, about the social media posts from Helicity soon after.

"C'mon." He guided her away from a group of teens giving her the side eye to the parking lot. "I'll give you a lift home."

"Are you sure you dare to be seen with me?" she muttered as she slipped into the seat next to him.

He gave a snort of laughter. "You know, plenty of people here would question why *you* dare to be seen with *me*." When she threw him a questioning look, he shrugged and started the engine. "Not everyone here sees me the way you do, Fifteen. Something I did back in freshman year earned me a reputation that's still clinging to me like skunk stink."

"What did you do?"

He made a face. "Pulled the fire alarm to get out of a final exam I hadn't studied for."

Helicity's eyes widened. "Were you expelled?"

"No, but only because it was the end of the school year. The other students were psyched by the interruption until they realized they had to stay late to retake the test." He gave a rueful smile. "Word of advice: if you want to be popular, don't prolong the last day of school. Anyway. I failed the exam and the course and had to go to summer school to make up for it." He cocked an eyebrow. "Three guesses who my teacher was."

"Wait—Lana?"

Sam nodded.

"I always wondered how you two met. Lana only said it was in school." She gave a small laugh. "So, my brother was right when he said you were trouble."

"Andy said that?"

"Yeah, before our storm-chasing trip with Lana and Ray. Told me I should steer clear of you."

Sam stopped for a red light and turned to look at her. "And yet here you are."

"Yeah," she replied, holding his gaze. "Here I am."

A frisson of energy passed between them. Then the light turned green, the car behind them honked, and Sam turned his attention back to the road. "Another piece of advice, for what it's worth? Don't read those social media posts. And don't answer them. That'll only make everything drag on longer. Those people bashing Andy will move to the next piece of gossip soon enough. Then things will get better."

Helicity wasn't sure Sam was right, but she followed his advice anyway. It didn't help. That evening while she was slicing cucumbers for salad, the buzz around Andy grew louder, more insistent, and more hurtful. Someone accused him of stealing the Michigan State athletic scholarship from more worthy, "clean and sober" candidates. A rival from another town hinted his outstanding high school football career was the result of taking performance-enhancing drugs. A third person suggested he'd faked his accident to gain access to opioids.

That last comment pushed her over the edge. Furious, she threw down the paring knife, snatched up her phone, and thumbed out a reply.

> My brother risked his life searching for me during the tornado! His car accident was REAL. His injuries are REAL. And he's got the steel rods in his arm to prove it!

The moment she hit POST, she regretted it. Her words unleashed a new string of comments. And this time, she was in the crosshairs.

> Why were you out in the tornado???

> I'll tell you why. Because she's a complete weather nut!

> What kind of name is Helicity?

> Get this: it's a weather term, means to spin! LOL

> Wait, wasn't she in a flash flood too?

> OMG, that's right! What's WITH her?

> Told you she was a nut. Emphasis on NUT.

A series of *LOL*s and crying-with-laughter emojis followed that last comment.

But Helicity wasn't laughing. She was rigid with frustration.

She was no saint—she'd made biting remarks about people behind their backs more than once, most recently about a girl named Cyn who'd flirted outrageously with Sam in Texas. And she wasn't foolish enough to believe she'd never been a target herself, even before the rumors about Andy started whirling. But the casual way these people were speculating about her, the downright *nastiness* of it, took her breath away.

And then the conversation crossed a line.

> I heard she almost drowned a lady professor in that flood.

CHAPTER FOURTEEN

*N*o! Helicity screamed inwardly. Her heart pounded, remembering Ray's warning that Lana needed to be free of stress. *Leave her out of it!*

She wanted to type those words in all caps. But she'd learned her lesson: don't give them any ammunition, because they'll fire it right back at you. To avoid the temptation, she shoved her phone to the far end of the island and grabbed the paring knife.

"Whoa, careful there!" Mrs. Dunlap came into

the kitchen just as Helicity took a vicious slash at the cucumber. She put her hand over Helicity's to stop her from slicing again. "What's going on?"

Helicity's desire to shield her mother from the gossip warred with her need for her guidance. Need won out, and she blurted out the whole story.

"And now, just because I defended Andy, people started making fun of me," she finished, her voice hitching with mounting anger. "What am I supposed to do if they turn on Lana, too? She's still so weak, Mom. If she found out what was being said about her . . ."

Her mother said nothing. Instead, she removed the knife from Helicity's grasp, scooped the cucumber slices into a container, and put the container in the refrigerator. "Dinner prep can wait." She moved to the door to the garage, car keys in hand. "Come on."

"Where are we going?" Helicity asked as they drove away from the house.

"You'll see."

Fifteen minutes later, Mrs. Dunlap pulled up to the ruins of a farmhouse, another wreck left behind by the tornado. Yellow caution tape roped off its gaping cellar hole. Only the barn, weathered gray by the elements, remained. Lights shone from within it, and when Helicity opened her car door, she heard rock music. Mystified, she waited while her mother retrieved a duffel bag from the trunk, then followed her inside.

The barn might have once held animals or farm machinery, but no more. With the music's throbbing beat pulsing through her body, she took in her surroundings. On one wall, a balding man did chin-ups on an adjustable bar. Next to him, an overweight woman puffed on a treadmill. Another woman grunted with exertion while flipping a huge tractor tire, and two men slapped long black ropes as thick as Helicity's forearm against the floor. Hand weights, dumbbells, floor mats, a rowing machine, and a heavy punching bag—all were in use by people of various shapes, sizes, and ages.

"Hold on," Helicity said. "Is this a gym?"

"It's a space for people to let off steam," a voice from behind her replied.

Helicity spun to find a sandy-haired man in a tank top and gym shorts grinning at her. "Pete!" Pete was a local police officer. After the tornado hit, he reunited

Helicity with her parents and later drove them to the hospital where Andy was undergoing surgery on his arm.

He shook her hand warmly. "It's great to see you, Helicity." He smiled at Mrs. Dunlap. "You, too. It's been a few weeks."

Helicity gave her mother an incredulous look. "You come here to exercise?"

"To let off steam, like Pete said." She pulled out a pair of pink fingerless boxing gloves from her duffel bag. "Want to give it a try?"

"Give *what* a try?"

In response, Pete motioned her to a side area. There, he took two oval focus pads from a rack of equipment, put one on each hand, and held them up at Helicity's shoulder height. "Put on the gloves. And then punch it out."

Helicity shook her head. "I don't think—"

Mrs. Dunlap pressed the gloves on her. "Don't think. Just do."

With reluctance, Helicity pulled on the gloves and tightened the Velcro straps around her wrists. "So now I just . . . what?"

"Now you hit the pads, like this." Her mother demonstrated, cross-punching one bare-knuckled fist at a focus pad, then the other fist at the opposite pad. After ten hits, she stepped aside and waved Helicity to her place.

Helicity shrugged self-consciously. "Okay, here goes nothing." She thrust out her fist and connected lightly with the pad. The impact vibrated up her arm but not in a bad way.

"Again," Mrs. Dunlap instructed.

"And hit as hard as you want," Pete added with a grin. "I can take it."

Helicity punched again. First one pad, then the other. Slowly and lightly. Clumsily, too, until she synchronized her movements to the thumping music. Once she found her rhythm, the punches flew faster and harder, her arms pumping out and in, side to side, one-two, one-two.

"Good! Good!" Pete encouraged. "Let it out, Helicity! Let it out!"

She struck the pads several more times, then, gasping, dropped her hands at her sides and stepped back.

"How do you feel?" her mother asked.

Helicity blinked. It was warm inside the barn and sweat was trickling down her back and turning the ends of her hair into points. Her heart was pounding. Her breathing was ragged.

Is this how Mia feels when she runs? she wondered. If so, then she was even happier her friend had found cross-country. Because punching against those pads had made her feel—

"Better," she said wonderingly. "I feel better." She brought her hands up into ready position. "Can I go again?"

As she launched into another round of punches, Mrs. Dunlap left to change into her workout gear. She exercised with a set of hand weights while Pete showed Helicity how to kick against the hanging heavy bag. Then she and her mother took turns on the rowing machine and the treadmill before calling it quits.

In the car, Helicity mopped perspiration from her face with the hem of her T-shirt. "So, that was fun. But when . . . ?"

"Did I start working out?" her mother supplied. "Not long after you left on the storm-chasing trip." She flicked a quick look at Helicity. "Full disclosure: I was a mess after the tornado. Jumping at every little sound. Panicking when the sky turned cloudy. Lashing out at your dad for working such long hours. Worrying about Andy." The words came out in a rush now. "It just got worse after you left on the storm-chasing trip. After the flash flood. After you went to Texas. After Andy vanished without a word. I wasn't sleeping. Tuning out at work. Eating nothing but fast food and chocolate. I was on a slippery slope toward a dark hole when I ran into Pete. He invited me to give his gym a try. Dad, too, though he only went a few times."

"Oh, Mom. I didn't realize . . ."

Her mother shook her head. "You weren't supposed to, darling. I was trying to be strong, but really, I was making myself weak by ignoring my emotions.

"Anyway," she continued, "punching and kicking those pads that first time loosened the knots in my stomach. So I went back. A few nights a week, then every night. Exercise, and the rush of endorphins that comes with it, helped me climb out of the darkness. So did weekly sessions with my therapist, by the way." She smiled at Helicity's surprised look. "Told you—full disclosure."

They pulled into the driveway, but neither got out of the car. "About those posts, Hel . . . we can't control what other people say or do. We can only control how we react to it. Right now, Sam's advice to stay silent seems sound."

"And in the meantime," Helicity added, "we can take our frustrations out at Pete's place."

"Or go for long horse rides," her mother agreed. "And if you want to meet with my therapist, just say the word."

Back inside, they showered, then curled up on the sectional with salads and garlic bread and binge-watched episodes of their favorite television show. For those few hours, a feeling of normalcy settled over them like a shared blanket.

But upstairs on her desk, Helicity's phone silently vibrated with notifications. Again. And again. And again.

CHAPTER FIFTEEN

"*H*elicity!" Lana's scream sliced through the air.

Helicity deepened and slowed her breathing. Clutched her necklace and reminded herself that it was just a voice on a video. The real Lana was resting quietly at home.

The original version of the video had been taken weeks earlier by a storm chaser named Tornado Tom. He and his partner had arrived at the scene of the flash flood moments after Helicity and Sam's SUV nose-dived into the river. Tom's dashboard camera captured Helicity helping a bloodied Sam to safety, her own struggle to secure herself to a towline, and the sound of Ray's truck roaring up.

But the clip that appeared on social media Wednesday night showed none of that. Whoever had posted it had doctored the video. Now it started with Lana's terrified scream, then cut to her racing into the dangerously frothing floodwaters to rescue Helicity. It showed Helicity clutching her with desperation. Then somehow, the video's creator had zoomed in on the moment Helicity's fingers slipped from Lana's shirt. The last scene showed Lana being swept away in the churning waves.

Helicity's eyes brimmed with tears, and not just for Lana. *It wasn't like that,* she wanted to scream. *Tom, Ray . . . they yanked my towline so hard I lost my grip on her shirt.* She had tried to upload Tornado Tom's full video to the post, but his website refused to allow it. How the person who manipulated the video had gotten hold of it, she had no clue; he or she must have had much more advanced computer skills than she had. What she did know was that her online protests would do little or nothing to counteract the doctored video's twisted truth, and might make the situation even worse.

"Why don't you reach out to Tornado Tom directly?" Mia suggested when they talked that night. "Or have Ray or Lana explain what really happened?"

"No way," Helicity said. "I can't involve Lana, not while she's still recovering. According to Tornado Tom's website, he's off chasing storms in a remote part of the world. In other words, unreachable."

"And Ray?"

"Hates social media. When he heard Lana was part of the mess, he cursed and told me to keep them both out of it." Helicity rolled onto her back and stared at her ceiling. "So I'm going to keep following Sam's advice and not say anything."

"Okay," Mia said. "If you're sure." But her tone indicated she thought it was a mistake.

And the next morning at school, Helicity thought so, too. Two days earlier, when Andy had been the object of gossip, people had shot knowing glances at her. Now they stared. Their whispers lingered when she walked by. Their hidden giggles changed to outraged huffs. She held her head high, but inside, she was crumbling.

Her mother was suffering, too, but unlike Helicity, the school pariah, she was the object of pity at work. Good-intentioned people greeted her with puckered foreheads and consoling touches that "made her skin crawl," she said. The only bit of good fortune they had was that, so far, word had not reached her father. Mrs. Dunlap refused to tell him for the same reason Helicity refused to tell Lana—the belief that the pain of knowing would cause far more damage.

Besides, she and her mother reasoned Thursday afternoon, it would likely all blow over before he and Andy returned home.

But they had underestimated the power of social media. Thursday night, the doctored flash-flood video showed up on a popular platform. By Friday, it had gone viral. Then the clip of Cheryl Wiggins's show popped up. And out of nowhere, an earlier television interview with a teenage girl named Summer surfaced. Summer and her two friends had ridden out the terrifying Texas derecho with Helicity, Mia, Trey, and Sam in an abandoned lakeside cabin. One of the boys had suffered lacerations to his face when a nearby window exploded. Trey had almost died from blood loss when a tree crashed through the roof and a thick branch pierced his thigh. And in the early minutes of that storm, Mia had nearly drowned after her sailboat's boom sent her flying overboard. Helicity had jumped in after her and hauled her aboard Summer's boat, but Summer made no mention of that in her interview or in the scathing comments about Helicity she added below the clip.

Social media went nuts. FOUR DIFFERENT STORMS! the headline screamed. FOUR NEAR-FATAL TRAGEDIES! ONE COMMON DENOMINATOR: HELICITY DUNLAP!

"We have to let Dad know," Mrs. Dunlap said Friday evening.

But he already knew. His voice blasted through the phone when he called at his usual time, his fury with social media almost as strong as his frustration with his wife and daughter for thinking they could shield him from its reach.

"We were going to start home, but now I don't know if we should," he spat. "Better we stay here, where only a handful of people know who Andy is, than to walk into the pit of snakes waiting for him there."

Mrs. Dunlap tearfully agreed. After they hung up, she scrubbed her exhausted face with her hands and turned to Helicity. "I've been thinking. Maybe we should get out of town for a few days."

"And go where?" Helicity asked miserably.

"Somewhere where we don't know anyone."

Sam was the one who came up with their destination. "ArtExpo in Chicago."

ArtExpo was a two-week-long cultural celebration that transformed downtown Chicago into a mecca of artistic talent. Artists from all over the world displayed their paintings, sculptures, photographs, and installations in coffee shops and historic houses, churches, and museums, even the bridges that crossed the Chicago River and the waterfront that bordered Lake Michigan.

"My dad always books a couple of rooms, just in case out-of-town friends want to come," Sam told her. "No one could make it this time, so they're ours if we want them. And Dad can't come either, unfortunately, because he has to work."

Mrs. Dunlap was all in favor of the getaway. So, the next morning, she and Helicity picked up Sam. As they drove out of town, Helicity felt the tension she'd been carrying for the past days start to ease. When she heard her mother singing along to the radio, she knew she was feeling more relaxed, too.

Three hours later, they parked at the hotel and made their way toward the downtown. It was a warm, crystal-clear September day, perfect for strolling the streets and dipping in and out of different venues. Normally, Helicity wasn't a fan of crowds. But now she welcomed the anonymity they gave her. For the next two days, she would be just another person enjoying the world of art.

Sam proved to be an expert guide. He'd mapped out a route the night before that took them to the most popular sites and more out-of-the-way places, too. Helicity was drawn to sculpture and outdoor installations, while her mother preferred modern paintings with lots of interesting details.

Sam, an avid amateur photographer, sought out photographs. In the halls of one wood-beamed office building their first morning, he beckoned Helicity over to look at a snowscape drenched purple, orange, and red from a brilliant sunset. "Says here the artist mounted the photo on metal instead of canvas because it makes the colors more vibrant," he said, reading a card near the image. "Huh. I'll have to remember that."

"You should enter some of your storm photos next time," Helicity commented. "You've got some amazing shots."

Sam shrugged. "You could, too, when you turn eighteen. Those photos of the Memorial Day tornado are great."

"Thanks, but photography is your thing, not mine. I'll stick to studying the weather, not filming it. You know, walking around with my head in the clouds, as my dad says." She offered up a smile.

He grinned back. A second later, he slapped himself on the forehead. "Dang it, Fifteen, I keep forgetting! I found your lightning bolt photo in the trunk of my car, underneath my camping gear."

"Oh, Sam, that's awesome!" Helicity's eyes shone. "I thought I'd lost it in the hurricane."

"I'm happy to report it made it home from Bolivar

safe and sound." He turned to look at her fully. "And happier that it means that much to you."

Butterflies suddenly took flight in her stomach as she returned his gaze. Then Sam blinked and, with a mumble, moved off to inspect the next piece of art. As Helicity's racing pulse slowed to normal, her mother called out from another part of the building. "Helicity! Helicity, come see this one!"

Helicity took a step back without looking and accidentally collided with a woman who had stepped forward at the same moment.

"Oh, I'm so sorry!" Helicity apologized. Then she blinked.

Helicity didn't normally take much notice of strangers. But this woman had caught her attention earlier because she wore sunglasses inside the building and a baseball cap pulled low over her eyes. More than that, though, something about the woman seemed oddly familiar.

The sense of familiarity increased when the woman smiled at her. "No harm done," she replied.

Everything clicked when the woman spoke. Helicity had only heard her voice once before, and through the filter of a television. But she recognized it instantly. "You—you're Cheryl Wiggins."

The woman's smile broadened. "Busted." She removed her sunglasses, glanced around as if to confirm they were alone, then leaned in close and whispered, "And you're Helicity Dunlap."

CHAPTER SIXTEEN

Helicity's jaw dropped. "How do you know my name?"

Cheryl drew herself up tall as if offended. "I'm a skilled investigative reporter. It's my job to know things." Then she relaxed and chuckled. "The truth is, I overheard you and your friend talking about the Bolivar hurricane. Also, that woman, who I assume is your mother"—she jerked her head toward Mrs. Dunlap—"called you *Helicity*. With such an unusual name, it didn't take much to put two and two

together and come up with the girl who saved Scout."
She held out her hand. "It's a real pleasure to meet you.
All of you," she added when Mrs. Dunlap and Sam
joined them.

Trying not to look starstruck, Helicity shook her
hand and introduced Sam and her mother.

"What are you doing here in Illinois, Ms. Wiggins?"
Mrs. Dunlap asked.

"Please, call me Cheryl. I'm here for the same reason you are—ArtExpo. A few up-and-coming artists
from Texas entered their work, and I'm profiling them
for my show. First, though, I wanted to get a feel for
the event without the cameras following me. I have to
say, I'm impressed."

"We are, too," Mrs. Dunlap agreed. "And Sam here
has been an excellent tour guide."

Cheryl eyed him. "Is that so? You know, I could use
an excellent tour guide. And I wouldn't mind some
company. Would it be okay if I tagged along with you
for a few hours?"

Helicity, Sam, and Mrs. Dunlap exchanged delighted
looks. "Of course!" Helicity's mother answered for all
of them.

Cheryl put her sunglasses back on. "Then what are we waiting for? Lead on, Sam!"

Helicity was a little tongue-tied around Cheryl at first. But the television star's down-to-earth manner soon put her at ease. Cheryl asked interesting questions that went beyond the usual "where are you from, what grade are you in, what's your favorite subject" queries many adults defaulted to. And she had a way of turning a question into a conversation. After Cheryl asked if she preferred Lake Michigan to the Gulf of Mexico, Helicity suddenly found herself talking about Scar, the dolphin that had stranded itself on the Bolivar Peninsula shore.

Cheryl listened raptly to the story of the dolphin's rescue. "So saving animals isn't limited to dogs for you," she commented. "Scar's lucky you were there that day. I hope he's okay."

"He was the last time I saw him." Helicity told her about visiting the marine animal rescue facility where Scar was recovering. "He was supposed to be released back into the wild. But then the hurricane hit, so I don't know if it happened. Or if the facility even made it through the storm." Her insides twisted at the thought of Scar and the other rescues trapped in their pools as the raging hurricane rained rubble down around them.

Cheryl paused in the middle of the sidewalk, then pulled out her phone and pressed a number. Holding up a "wait a moment" finger, she walked a few paces away and had a rapid conversation with someone on the other end. When she turned back, she switched the finger for a thumbs-up. "My assistant Keith tells me Scar was released in plenty of time to head for open waters," she said, hanging up, "and that the facility came through the storm relatively unscathed."

"How did he—? Never mind." Helicity didn't care how Keith found his information. She just wanted to pass it along. "I have to make sure Trey knows!" Thumbs dancing over the keys, she sent him a text. Moments later, he replied with a big smiley face emoji. A second message followed.

> U OK?

With those three letters, Helicity's happiness flagged. She'd communicated with Trey a few times in the past week. They'd talked about a lot of things—school, Mia's running, her new exercise routine—but never about the social media posts. She'd hoped that, somehow, he hadn't seen them. But now she knew he had.

Yeah, she replied. *I'm OK.*

> Want to talk?

Thanks. Maybe another time, though? I'm at an art show with—she paused, flicked a look from Sam to Cheryl, and decided not to mention either of them—*my mom.*

Anytime, came Trey's instant reply. *Have fun being all cultural!*

She closed out the message, her good mood returning. She and Trey hadn't parted on perfect terms. But through texts and occasional phone calls, they were slowly rebuilding their friendship. It felt good knowing he was on her side.

After an hour wandering the streets by the waterfront, Cheryl declared she was starving and insisted on buying them lunch. They chose food trucks and a shaded picnic table over a crowded indoor restaurant.

Midway through the meal, Cheryl set her sandwich aside, dabbed at her mouth with her napkin, and fixed her gaze on Helicity. "I have a confession to make. I've been following you on social media."

Everybody else stopped eating. Then Sam thrust away his plate. "Are you kidding me? Is that why you asked to hang out with us? So you could dig up dirt on Helicity for your show?"

"Sam," Mrs. Dunlap cautioned, though her frown was for Cheryl.

Cheryl held up her hands. "It's a fair question. My answer is a definite no." She reached across the table and touched Helicity's arm. "You think I don't know what it's like to be the object of hateful and hate-filled comments?" She shook her head. "I know only too well. And that's a big reason why I've worked very hard to be a different sort of 'celebrity.'" She put air quotes around the word, as if wanting to distance herself from the term.

"So exactly what kind of 'celebrity'"—Sam imitated her air quotes sarcastically—"are you?"

"The decent kind, I hope." Cheryl sighed. "I'm not stupid. I know scandal sells and insults grab headlines. But that's not me. I seek out the stories that lift people up, that make their hearts feel full, that give them a reason to trust fellow human beings. Stories like the one Scout's owner, Charles Bainbridge, shared."

"Okay, I can get behind that," Sam said grudgingly. "But what's your interest in Helicity?"

"It's not just *my* interest, Sam." Cheryl regarded Helicity. "You've captured the public's eye, Helicity, but not in the way you deserve. Being mentioned on my show has played into that. When I found out about the posts, I felt responsible for adding to your pain. So I asked Keith to keep tabs on the situation. And yes, to learn what he could about you."

"Learn about me?" Helicity echoed faintly, squeezing her napkin into a tight, sweat-moistened ball in her lap. "Why?"

Cheryl leaned over the table, trying to catch her eye. "Because I believed there was something more to the girl who risked her life for a helpless dog. Who survived on her own without food and little water during one of the worst hurricanes the Gulf Coast has seen in decades. Who faced other disasters, too, and emerged in one piece. I believed there was more to the girl than what the gossips were saying. So when we met today—a total, happy coincidence, by the way—I jumped at the chance to discover for myself the person you are."

"And? What kind of person am I?" Helicity lifted her chin defiantly. But a small part of her was curious, too.

Cheryl cocked her head to one side. "Strong. Smart. Caring. Brave. Daring, even. And I think, I *hope*—"

The chime of her cell phone interrupted whatever she was about to add. Her eyes darted across the screen, then she looked up with a smile.

"I *hope*," she finished, "that you're the kind of person who likes adventure and meeting new people. Because if so, I have an opportunity to offer you." She gestured at her phone. "After being on my show, Charles Bainbridge told me he wanted to reward you for what you did for his daughter. Earlier, I asked Keith to reach out to him, to let him know I was with you. Keith now tells me that Charles has offered to fly you and a chaperone"—she nodded at Mrs. Dunlap—"to Albuquerque, to be their guest during the opening weekend of the International Balloon Fiesta."

Helicity was struck dumb. "I didn't rescue Scout to earn a reward," she finally said.

"I know. They know. But Charles wasn't kidding when he said you saved Tabitha that day. If Scout had died, he believes her anguish could have overwhelmed her." She nodded at Mrs. Dunlap. "You're a parent. If someone went above and beyond to help your child, wouldn't you want to thank them?"

Helicity's mother flicked a glance at Sam. Helicity knew she was remembering how Sam had saved Andy. How he'd tried to save her. "I would," she said softly.

They fell silent for a moment, then Sam asked, "Um, what's a balloon fiesta? Like, a big celebration with birthday party balloons?"

Cheryl laughed. "A big celebration, yes, but with hot-air balloons. Hundreds of them, actually. They fill the skies near Albuquerque from dawn to dusk for nine days in early October. I've been told it's absolutely spectacular."

Helicity's pulse quickened as she imagined the scene. "And we could go?" She directed this question at her mother.

Mrs. Dunlap opened her mouth. Closed it. "Maybe, Hel," she said at last. "That's the best answer I can give right now," she added to Cheryl.

"Of course," Cheryl responded. "But if you decide to go, there could be more to the visit. With your permission, yours and Helicity's, I would like to livestream your meeting with Charles and Tabitha for my show." She captured Helicity's gaze and held it. "I would also like to give you the chance to set the record straight. There are many sides to every story. But only the sides that get told are heard. So tell your story. Let people see that Helicity Dunlap is more than what social media has painted her to be."

Helicity stared, her mind whirling. What Cheryl was proposing was more than she could process at that moment. So she simply repeated what her mother had said. "Maybe. That's the best answer I can give right now."

"I can get behind that," Cheryl said with a wink at Sam. "In the meantime, I have one last question for you. For all of you. Did you, or did you not"—she jerked a thumb at a nearby street vendor—"save room for ice cream?"

CHAPTER SEVENTEEN

Helicity spent the rest of the weekend at Art-Expo in a daze. She saw Cheryl only once more, when she was filming an interview with one of the Texas artists. She didn't think Cheryl saw her, though, not with the crowd of curious bystanders flocking around her. But that didn't matter. She had Cheryl's contact information on her phone and a request to give her an answer for Mr. Bainbridge within the week.

"I hope you'll say yes," Cheryl said when they parted

company after ice cream. "But if not, send me a note now and then so I know how you're doing, okay?"

The ride back home Sunday afternoon was mostly silent. Sam perked up when they dropped him off at his house.

"Hang on a sec, okay?" He disappeared inside, returning a minute later with a flat, rectangular package wrapped in brown paper. "Your lightning photo," he said as he slipped the package through the window into Helicity's waiting hands. "And something else, too, that I hope you like."

Helicity tore open the paper as Mrs. Dunlap backed out of the driveway. On top was her birthday photo, the lightning a brilliant jagged streak across the dark, cloudy sky. Her fingers crept to her necklace as she read what he'd written on the back:

You'll return Lana's lightning bolt someday.
But this one is yours to keep.

Tucked beneath that photo was another, unframed print. Helicity's breath caught in her throat when she saw the sun-splashed shot of the Bolivar lighthouse.

A larger version of the photo had once hung in the Beachside. Background details—a patch of grass, palm trees, a house on stilts—had matched fleeting images she'd seen during her last video call with Andy. Those details had spurred her frantic bike ride to the lighthouse to search for him. To the lighthouse that became her prison for nearly two days.

An unexpected wave of panic triggered by the photo suddenly threatened to overwhelm her. *Get a grip, Helicity! It's just a picture.* Still, she breathed easier after she flipped the image facedown.

That's when she saw Sam had written on the back of this photo, too. Just three words:

Still standing strong.

Her anxiety slowly ebbed. *Still standing strong. Does he mean me or the lighthouse?* She pulled out her phone to text him the question, then paused and turned the photo over again. With Sam's words dancing in her mind, she saw the lighthouse in a new way. Not as her prison, but as the edifice that saved her life. And she saw herself through his eyes: still standing strong. As they drew near their house, she tapped Sam a text as simple and straightforward as his inscription:

> I love the lighthouse. Thanks.

She'd just hit SEND when her mother made a puzzled sound in her throat. "Whose car is that?"

Helicity looked up—and gasped. "The beach-mobile!"

"It's the *what*?"

"The beach-mobile!" Helicity scrambled out before their car came to a stop. "Suze's car!"

The beach-mobile was Mia's aunt's pride and joy. A convertible from a bygone era, it was as long as a limo, as wide as a bus, and painted a bright turquoise that contrasted beautifully with the chrome trim and white rag top. In Texas, the beach-mobile had drawn stares. But in Michigan, birthplace of the US automobile industry, it would be the envy of all who saw it, even with the dents and scratches left by the hurricane.

"Suze? Suze?" Helicity hollered as she tore up the steps.

The front door opened. A tall figure stepped into the fading afternoon light. His muscles weren't as toned as they'd once been, and his face was haggard. But his eyes, the same sea green as Helicity's, were clear and bright. And his lopsided grin held a hint of its former mischief.

"I've been called lots of things," he drawled. "But never a girl's name."

"*Andy!*" Helicity hurled herself into her brother's waiting embrace. Clung to him even as her mother burst into tears and wrapped her arms around them both. "Oh, Andy. You're back. You're really, really back."

"Yeah," he murmured. "Thanks to you."

Mr. Dunlap appeared then and ushered them into the living room. On the coffee table was a platter of cheese and crackers, a bowl of grapes, and—

"Andy's candy dish!" Helicity gaped at the misshapen yellow-green bowl filled with wrapped sweets. "But it was lost in the tornado!"

Smiling, her father rapped the bowl with his knuckles. "This thing is indestructible, apparently. I unearthed it in the wreckage. I was waiting for the right time to bring it out. This seemed as good a time as any."

Mrs. Dunlap examined it more closely. "Oh, no. It's got a chip in it." She ran her finger around the rim.

"One more thing the storm left damaged," Helicity's father muttered.

A shadow crossed Andy's face. Helicity realized her father's words had deeper meaning for him. "Dad," she whispered.

"What?" Then Mr. Dunlap saw Andy's face, too. "Oh. I didn't mean—"

"I know you didn't," Andy interrupted. He stood up, shoved his hands in his pockets, and rocked on his heels. The pink-and-white post-surgery scars on his right arm stood out against his tan. But that wasn't the damage he meant. "But we're all thinking the same thing. That the tornado left me damaged, too. And it's true. I've been to the bottom of a dark hole. I'm crawling my way out. But I've got a long way to go yet. Which is why I'll be going to support meetings every day. Twice a day if I need to."

Andy sat back down. Helicity leaned against him, only half listening as her father answered her mother's questions about how they came to make the journey

home in the beach-mobile. "I helped dig out the car. When Andy got out of the clinic, Suze handed me the keys. And here we are."

Helicity suspected there was more to the story but didn't press. She didn't ask why they'd decided to come home instead of stay in Texas, away from the whispers and glances, either. She was just glad they'd made that decision, and from the happiness on their faces, she was certain they were, too.

Soon after, Andy gave a huge yawn and announced he needed a rest. She went to her room, too. After unpacking her overnight bag and propping her new photos next to the tornado one, she opened her laptop and searched for information on the International Balloon Fiesta.

What she found intrigued her. The images and videos of the balloons drifting through the sky were even more spectacular than Cheryl had described. What would it be like to see those floating giants in person? she wondered. Or to ride in the basket of one as it took flight?

Despite her interest, Helicity was hesitant to take

Mr. Bainbridge up on his offer. He was a complete stranger, after all, and staying with him might be awkward. Then there was the flight to New Mexico. Her one experience on a plane had not been pleasant. As for telling her side of the story on Cheryl's show . . . what could she possibly say that would change people's minds about her?

Helicity dozed off with these thoughts jumbled in her mind. When she woke a few hours later, it was night. She padded into the hallway and veered toward the open bathroom door—then jumped back with a startled cry.

Andy stood at the sink. The lights were off, but she could see he had a glass in one hand. In the other, he had a bottle of pills. He turned at her cry. "Hel? Everything okay?"

Her eyes darted to the pills. He followed her gaze. His face contorted with sorrow. "Oh." He opened his palm. "Over-the-counter pain medication. For a headache. See for yourself."

"I believe you."

Andy set down the glass and turned on the light. She blinked against the harsh brightness as he shook a few pills into his hand. "See for yourself," he repeated.

The tablets were long and white and stamped with the name of a popular pain reliever. "Okay."

He returned all but two to the bottle, then downed the dosage with the water. "It's not like last time, Hel," he said quietly. "Not like when you caught me with Mia's pills. I needed you to see that."

"Okay," she said again.

Andy clicked off the light but didn't move. She didn't, either. "That night on the beach was the turning point," he said, his voice still soft. "The look on your face, the way I screamed at you, my complete desperation . . ." He shook his head. "I've never hated myself more than at that moment. That's why I ran."

"Right to Johnny," she murmured before she could stop herself. "Sam and I, we heard it all through his dashboard camera."

Andy stared at the floor. "Oh."

"But we also heard you refuse to stay behind and rob the homes of people who'd evacuated the peninsula ahead of the hurricane," she quickly added. "After that, we lost contact. What happened?"

"Johnny and I fought. I landed a few punches and got the camera from him. He took off in his car. I drove around for a while, then left Sam's car at the Beachside and wandered around on foot. I slept in the lighthouse. When I woke up, I made a phone call."

"To me."

"No. That came later. My first call was to the police."

Helicity flashed back to the newspaper article Kate had posted. "The anonymous tip about Johnny. It was from you?"

Andy nodded. They were quiet for a moment. Then Andy sighed. "I've made such a mess of things, Hel."

"You're home now. Things will get better."

"Will they? Or will my return just make everything worse?" He glanced at her sideways. "I know people have been throwing some nasty shade at me. At us." He lowered his head into his hands. "What I don't know is how to make them stop. Because what they're saying—about me, anyway—is true."

Something Cheryl said came back to Helicity then: *There are many sides to every story. But only the sides that get told are heard.*

What would happen, she wondered, if Andy came out of the shadows and told his side of the story? She turned to her brother. "Do you trust me?"

He looked puzzled but nodded.

"Good. Because I have an idea."

CHAPTER EIGHTEEN

Mr. Dunlap dropped his spoon into his bowl of cereal with a loud clank. "You want to go to New Mexico to tell your story to this Cheryl Wiggins woman. And you want Andy to come with you instead of your mother. You want to put him on camera, too, and have him tell everyone that they were right. That he was addicted to painkillers." He spread his hands and shot his wife an incredulous look. "Am I the only one here who thinks this idea is insane?"

Helicity glanced at Andy. When she'd first proposed the plan the night before, he'd looked at her like she was crazy, too. Until she pointed out that saying nothing hadn't silenced their critics. Maybe honesty would.

"At least then Andy would be in control of the story," she said now.

Mrs. Dunlap shook her head. "Even if I thought it was a good idea, it's too soon. You need stability, structure, calm, Andy. Flying off to New Mexico won't provide that."

Andy made a face. "You think I'm going to have calm here, once people find out I'm back home?" When she wouldn't meet his eyes, he added, "It's just a couple of days, Mom. And I'll be with Hel the entire time." He elbowed Helicity. "If anyone can keep me in line, she can."

"If there's even a chance going on Cheryl's show can help us," Helicity put in, "shouldn't we take it?"

Helicity sensed her mother was wavering. Her father was harder to read. "I have to get to work," he said gruffly. "We'll talk about this more tonight."

Helicity spent the school day debating with herself

about which way her parents would decide. In the hall between classes, she was so preoccupied with her thoughts she didn't see Kate until the girl moved directly in her path.

"So, your brother's back in town, huh?" She smiled at Helicity's stunned look. "Don't bother denying it. Thanks to my cousin, I have proof." She waved her phone under Helicity's nose. On the screen was a blurry picture of Andy getting behind the wheel of the beach-mobile. "Nice car. Real classy. Wonder where he was going in it?" She raised her voice loud enough to draw the attention of the passing students. "To meet up with his drug dealer, maybe?"

Helicity slapped the phone aside. "Get out of my way, Kate," she hissed. "And stay away." She stormed into class with Kate's mocking laughter ringing in her ears—and even greater conviction that her idea of Andy telling his story made sense.

"Is Kate spying on me or something?" Andy said in disbelief when Helicity told him of her encounter. "If so, she'd know I went to a support group meeting and then picked up some supplies at an automotive store to help fix Suze's car."

Helicity wrinkled her nose. "Since when do you know anything about fixing cars?"

"I don't," Andy admitted. "Luckily, I found a guy who does."

Before Helicity could ask who, the doorbell rang. She blinked in surprise when she saw who was on the other side. "Ray? What're you doing here? Is Lana okay?"

"She's just fine. We can go see her when we're done if you want." Ray looked past her to Andy. "You ready?"

Helicity's jaw dropped. "Wait a minute. *Ray* is your car guy?"

Ray thumped his chest. "I've been working on classic automobiles since before they were classic. Inside and out."

"Sam told me about Ray on our drive to Texas," Andy added. "I got in touch with him last night."

"Enough chitchat," Ray said impatiently. "I'm itching to get my hands on that beauty in your driveway!"

For the next two hours, Helicity did her homework to the sound of pinging hammers, fizzing air compressors, and deep throaty laughter. Andy was sweaty and dirty when he came inside, but Helicity hadn't seen him so happy since before the tornado. "Ray's packing up his tools, then he's heading to Lana's. Said for us to come over after I shower."

"Us?"

Andy paused with his hand on the stair banister. "I thought it was time I thanked the woman who saved my sister's life."

Helicity swallowed back sudden tears. "I'll text Mom where we're going. And Andy?"

"Yeah?"

"Be sure to use lots of soap. You stink."

Twenty minutes later, Helicity had the odd sensation of worlds colliding as she watched Andy and Lana embrace. She was struck, too, by their similarities. Both had been weakened, physically and mentally. Both were struggling to regain their strength. And both were showing signs that they were winning their battles. Lana's cheeks had color, her eyes snapped with curiosity, and her movements hinted that her energy was returning. Andy's eyes were clear and focused, and he laughed easily. They weren't fully recovered yet. But they were inching closer.

The conversation quickly turned to the proposed

trip to Albuquerque. Helicity hadn't revealed Andy's secret to Lana and Ray. But to her shock, he did so himself just then, starting with his car accident and ending with his call to the Bolivar police and his stint in rehab. When he saw her staring at him, he gave a lopsided grin. "Figured I better test out my story among friends before I do it in front of a camera. How'd I do?"

Ray patted his leg. "You told it like it is, son. There is no better way to tell it."

"Say exactly what you said when you're on Cheryl's show, and you'll be fine," Lana added.

"If," Helicity corrected. "*If* we go on Cheryl's show. Dad said we'd talk more about it tonight, and I honestly have no clue what our parents' decision will be."

Lana looked thoughtful. "I convinced your mother to let you go on the storm-chasing trip. Perhaps I could convince her about this trip, too."

"What would you say, though?" Helicity asked doubtfully. "Last time, she agreed because you were going with me. This time, it'd just be Andy and me."

"Mmm." Lana drummed her fingers on the arm of the sofa. "Guess that means I'll have to go with you."

Helicity sat up. "What?"

"No. No way," Ray intervened. "Lana, you are—"

"Ready to stop being treated like an invalid!" Lana cut in forcefully. Then she softened her voice. "Ray, I love you, but you're smothering me with your constant hovering and worry. I need to get out of this house. I need to test myself. I need to . . . to *live*."

A hush fell over the room. Lana broke it. "If you're that worried about me, though, there is something you can do."

"Which is?" Ray asked.

Lana smiled. "Drive me to New Mexico. I want to see the countryside up close, not from a plane."

That night at dinner, Helicity and Andy laid out their revised plan for their parents. "We'll fly together," Helicity said with a nod at her brother. "Lana and Ray will drive there. They'll stay with Ray's friends and we'll stay with the Bainbridges. So except for traveling and sleeping, we'll be with Ray and Lana the entire time."

"Mr. Bainbridge, too," Andy added.

Their parents exchanged looks. For a heartbeat, Helicity was sure they'd refuse to let them go. Then her mother folded her napkin, laid it alongside her plate, and rested her hands on the table. "This summer has been incredibly stressful. For all of us. I had hoped that this fall, we'd find some semblance of peace. But these wretched videos and awful social media posts have stirred up even more trouble." She gazed at Helicity, then at Andy. "If you both truly believe that going to New Mexico, going on Cheryl's show, will help in some way, then I want you to go."

Helicity let out the breath she'd been unconsciously holding. They all turned to Mr. Dunlap.

He cleared his throat. "I made up my mind earlier today. Nothing you've said tonight has changed that."

Helicity's heart fell.

"Dad—" Andy started to say.

Mr. Dunlap held up his hand. "Let me finish. You haven't changed my mind"—he paused—"because I was already in favor of you going."

Helicity's mouth formed an O. "Really?" she squeaked.

"Yes. On one condition." He looked at Helicity and then at Andy. "Neither of you says anything about Andy's . . . problem."

"But that's the whole point of him going," Helicity blurted.

Her father sat back in his chair, looking suddenly exhausted. "The point of him going," he said quietly, "is to get this mess under control. This Cheryl woman is all about feel-good stories, right? So that's what you give her." He pointed at Andy. "You start with how you rushed out in a tornado to rescue your sister only to wind up in the hospital, your college hopes and dreams shattered. How you followed Helicity to Texas out of concern for her well-being and landed a job painting houses. How you became suspicious that another painter was dealing drugs and phoned in an anonymous tip that led to his arrest."

Helicity stared at her hands. Everything her father was saying was true. But it wasn't the whole truth. And that felt enough like lying to make her squirm. She said nothing, though. It was Andy's story. Therefore, it was his decision to make.

After a long moment, he made it.

CHAPTER NINETEEN

"**D**id you know Dad's afraid of flying?"

Helicity stopped fumbling with her lap belt to stare at her brother in the aisle seat. He nodded. "It's true. That's why he convinced Suze to let us drive the beach-mobile back to Michigan. He claimed it was because he knew someone who specialized in classic cars, but really, he's terrified of flying. Thinks the plane is going to crash."

Helicity's fingers crept to her necklace as she

remembered the turbulence that had rocked the one flight she'd ever taken. "Yeah, I get how he feels," she murmured.

It was two weeks after their discussion around the dinner table. After Andy, and then Helicity more reluctantly, had agreed to their father's condition. Afterward, Helicity had spent more than one sleepless night wondering if they had made the right decision.

Well, it's too late to turn back now, she thought as the plane roared down the runway.

Once they were in the air, Helicity pushed aside her misgivings. Flying with Andy helped. He was much more fun than the airline chaperone who'd accompanied her to Texas. They played cards, challenged each other in trivia, and shared candy and snacks they'd purchased in the airport. Still, after hours in the air and one too-quick stopover, Helicity was ready to get off the plane and stretch her legs.

Per arrangement, Mr. Bainbridge had sent a car to bring them to his house. Andy nudged Helicity as they walked off the skybridge. "Check it out." A woman was holding a sign marked DUNLAP. "We're famous." He stuck his nose in the air and sauntered to the driver with an exaggerated swagger that made Helicity roll her eyes and laugh.

Half an hour later, the car pulled off the main road onto a long, winding driveway. Helicity's eyes widened when she saw the house at the end. The sprawling adobe ranch was illuminated by soft solar lighting and landscaped with large cacti, desert plants, and rough-hewn boulders. It looked less like a house and more like a part of the desert landscape and distant mountain range that surrounded it. "It's so beautiful," she breathed.

The arched front doorway opened, and Mr. Bainbridge stepped out, waving his hand in greeting. "Helicity! Andy! Welcome, welcome, welcome!"

Helicity and Andy had communicated with Mr. Bainbridge via video chat and text since accepting his generous offer. He seemed as warm and friendly in person as he was over the phone.

A little dog darted out from behind his legs and met them on the walkway. "Scout!" Helicity knelt and ruffled the dog's ears and got a gentle lick on her cheek in return. "Hey, girl. Good to see you, too."

Scout gave a bark, then wheeled around and trotted

back inside. That's when Helicity noticed the young girl hiding behind Mr. Bainbridge. Tabitha, she realized. Mr. Bainbridge had chosen not to include his daughter in their video conversations, so this was the first time they'd met her. She looked small for her age. Helicity wanted to step forward and greet her. But she suddenly felt awkward. She didn't have much experience with little kids, not having any younger siblings or friends with little sisters or brothers. Plus, Tabitha had social anxiety. What if she said the wrong thing and set her off?

As she shifted uncomfortably from foot to foot, wondering what to do, Andy pulled a small rubber frog shaped like an hourglass from his backpack. "Dum-te-dum-te-dum," he hummed. "I wonder what would happen if I squeezed this—OH!"

As his fist tightened, the frog's eyes bugged out and the toy made a little squeak. "Well, that was weird! Probably it won't happen again—OH!" This time when the eyes bugged, Helicity heard a tiny giggle along with the squeak. Tabitha inched out from behind her father.

Andy feigned surprise. "Where did you come

from?" he asked, squatting down in front of her. "Never mind. I'm just glad you're here because I need someone to hold this for me. Thanks." He handed her the frog, then began rooting around in his backpack again.

Tabitha stared at the frog. Then with a shy glance at Andy, she tightened her grip. The eyes popped, the toy squeaked, and Andy's jaw dropped open. "Whoa!" he cried as if amazed. "You're strong! I was going to shake your hand, but now I'm afraid you might hurt me if I do."

"I won't," Tabitha said. Her voice was as small and shy as she was, but she was smiling. "I promise."

"Well, since you promise." Andy held out his hand. After a moment's hesitation, Tabitha took it. "You know this means we're friends now, right?" he said as they shook.

"We are?"

"Good friends," he emphasized. "Which is why I want you to keep that toy. And meet my sister, who is one of the greatest people I know."

Helicity finally found her voice. "Hi, Tabitha. I'm—"

"Helicity." Tabitha looked up at her with awe. "You're the girl in the lighthouse. You saved Scout." Without warning, she flung her arms around Helicity's waist. "You're one of the greatest people I know, too."

All Helicity's awkwardness vanished as she hugged Tabitha. The girl took her hand when they broke apart. "Come on. I'll show you where you'll be sleeping."

With Mr. Bainbridge and Andy trailing behind, Tabitha led her through a small interior courtyard open to the sky. Helicity craned her neck, admiring the view. Inside, they walked through the kitchen and dining room to a living room with a wall of windows. Through them, Helicity spotted a glimmering in-ground pool.

"You remembered your swimsuits, I hope?" Mr. Bainbridge queried. When Helicity and Andy nodded, he invited them to go for a dip after they unpacked.

The bedrooms themselves were small but comfortable with a shared bathroom in between. Helicity dug out her swimsuit, tossed a T-shirt on over it, and met Andy in the hallway.

"Where'd you get that frog toy?" she asked curiously.

He looked over his shoulder as if to make sure they were alone before answering. "At the treatment facility. It's a tool to remind me of . . . well, everything. Some people carry worry stones or wear bracelets they can snap against their wrists to help them through stressful moments. I chose the frog."

Helicity bit her lip. "Won't you need it, then?"

He smiled. "I've got you to remind me of what's important. Now come on. Let's swim."

After the long day of travel coupled with the swim and change in time zone—it was nine o'clock in New Mexico, but Helicity was still on Michigan time, where it was eleven—Helicity fell asleep the moment her head hit the pillow. Too soon, her alarm woke her. The clock read 4:00. With a growl, she started to roll over and go back to sleep. Then she remembered why she wanted to get up so early.

That morning, the Balloon Fiesta kicked off with an event called Mass Ascension, when more than six hundred hot-air balloons took to the sky in a single two-hour period. Mr. Bainbridge had promised it was

a sight not to be missed, even though it meant leaving home before sunrise.

It was still dark when they joined the throngs of people streaming into the main area of Balloon Fiesta Park. Tabitha held tight to Helicity's hand. Animals weren't allowed, otherwise Scout would have been with them, but she'd brought her new squeeze frog instead. "I don't like the dark, but I know I'll be safe with you," she said. Helicity gripped the little hand more firmly.

Inside the park, fully inflated balloons, their baskets resting on the ground, prepared to take flight. The quick *whoosh* of propane igniting into intense flames reminded Helicity of Scar's breath, only much louder. At precisely six o'clock, balloons began lifting off. Like bubbles in a glass of soda, they rose up and up and up, traveling to heights of more than four thousand feet above the ground. There, they drifted around the park in a wide circle, the dawn sunbeams making them glow like soft Christmas lights—and flashing brilliantly now and then when their pilots fired the burners again.

Helicity was transfixed. She longed to soar with

them, to feel her feet lift from the ground, weightless and flying free. Seeing the world from an airplane was thrilling. But floating through the sky in an open-air balloon, where, with a spin of her body, she could view everything in every direction for miles, could literally reach out and touch a passing cloud . . . that, she thought, would be magical.

A tap on her shoulder brought her back down to earth. She turned to see who was behind her. And nearly fell over in shock.

CHAPTER TWENTY

"**S**am? What are you doing here?"

Sam grinned. "Nice to see you, too." His gaze fell on Tabitha and his grin widened. "You're Tabitha, right?"

Tabitha ducked her head and edged behind Helicity.

"Hey, it's okay," Helicity said, giving Tabitha's shoulder a gentle squeeze. "This is just Sam. He's my . . . um, friend."

Tabitha gave her a keen look. "Friend? Like, boy-friend?"

Mercifully, Helicity was saved from answering by Ray and Lana's arrival. Lana was walking, not in the wheelchair she'd been using at home, though she leaned heavily on Ray's arm. They'd departed Michigan Thursday afternoon, Ray told her, and driven as far as they could before stopping for the night, then got up early Friday to drive the rest of the way to Albuquerque. Lana jerked a thumb at Sam. "As you can see, we picked up a stray before we left."

Andy and Mr. Bainbridge joined them. After introductions all around, Andy gave Sam a light punch in the arm. "You didn't play hooky from school on Friday, did you?"

"Me? Never. Seriously, though," Sam said, "I got an excused absence because I'm visiting a college."

Helicity noticed Andy flinched at the word *college*. She knew their father hoped he would enroll for the second semester at Michigan State and maybe even earn a place on the football team next fall. It was the main reason he'd insisted they both stay quiet about Andy's drug use. And why Andy had agreed to do so. Helicity wondered how he really felt, though.

Sam craned his neck upward. Dawn had softened

the black sky to a pale blue-gray, the perfect back-drop for the multicolored balloons. "But I would have skipped school for this. Man. It's . . . it's . . ."

"Really cool?" Tabitha supplied.

Sam smiled at her. "Ri*donk*ulously cool," he replied, earning him a smile from her and an amused eye roll from Helicity.

They stayed at the park until all the balloons had ascended, then Mr. Bainbridge announced he was ready for breakfast. Rather than battle the crowds for food on Main Street, he invited everyone back to his house.

In the parking lot, Helicity spotted Ray's truck right away. "You brought Mo West?" she said, laughing.

"Mo West?" Mr. Bainbridge asked.

"Stands for Mobile Weather Station. I outfitted her myself with all the high-tech equipment we storm chasers need," Ray explained proudly.

Helicity noticed with a flush of pleasure that he included Sam and her in that *we*.

"Storm chasers, eh?" Mr. Bainbridge chuckled. "Well, you won't need your equipment here, I'm happy to say. This time of year, the only wild weather we

get is the occasional thunderstorm. And I doubt we'll see one of those. In fact, it's been weeks since we had any rain. It falls from the clouds but never hits the ground."

Helicity nodded knowingly. "Virga."

Mr. Bainbridge looked confused. "Excuse me?"

With a smile at Helicity, Lana explained, "*Virga* is the meteorological term for rain that evaporates before it reaches the surface."

"Ah! That's right, you're a weather whiz." Mr. Bainbridge cocked an eyebrow. "So, tell me, do you know why this is such a prime location for ball-ooning?"

"I do, actually," Helicity replied. "It's because of the Albuquerque Box."

"The what?" Sam asked.

Ray blew a raspberry of disgust with his lips. "Some weather buff you are. Go ahead, Helicity. Tell him."

Helicity hesitated, not wanting to come off as a know-it-all. Sam nudged her with his elbow. "Don't leave me hanging!"

"Okay, okay! The Albuquerque Box is a weather phenomenon formed by the prevailing winds and the

surrounding landscape." Helicity held a hand palm-down near her waist. "Cold air from the mountains north of the city flows down here to the valley. It stays a few hundred feet above the ground. At the same time, warm air travels up from the south at a higher elevation. The currents blow in opposite directions, creating a two-level circular route of air—the Albuquerque Box." She held her other hand at shoulder height and demonstrated the airflow by moving her hands in circles.

"So, what's the connection between the Box and ballooning?" Andy wanted to know.

"Pilots move balloons up and down by increasing and decreasing the hot air inside them. They can't steer them, though. They rely on wind to push them sideways. That's where the Box comes in. The balloons lift off in the lower, cooler airflow. They ride that current to the south. At the same time, the pilots float them higher. High enough, and the balloons catch the warm air current, which pushes them northward. When the Albuquerque Box conditions are just right, the balloons can take off, circle around the park, and land near where they started."

The full explanation was a lot more complex, but Helicity didn't think a parking lot was the best place for an in-depth weather lesson. Plus, Sam was giving her an amused look, and she didn't want him to poke fun at her.

"I'm impressed." Mr. Bainbridge glanced at Lana. "Did you teach her that?"

"Helicity is self-taught," Lana answered with a hint of pride. "Though from time to time I'll add a little wisdom to her knowledge."

After a late breakfast in the Bainbridges' kitchen, they all relaxed by the pool. Helicity was dozing off in the warm sunshine when Scout's wet nose on her arm woke her. She petted her a few times, then glanced at her phone and saw she had a voice message.

"Hey, Helicity!" It was Cheryl. "I'm sending you a text with the final plans for tomorrow afternoon. Text me back if you have any questions. Okay?"

Helicity's heart bumped in her chest. She'd been so caught up in the morning events and Sam's unexpected appearance, she'd almost forgotten Cheryl was interviewing Andy and her the next day. Earlier in the week, Cheryl had supplied them each with a list of questions she was most likely to ask. "I should warn you, though," she added in a follow-up phone call, "I sometimes go off script. Meaning, if our conversation takes an interesting or unexpected turn, I might follow it, see where it goes. Those are usually my most rewarding interviews, for me, for my guest, and for viewers."

Helicity pulled up the questions on her phone now. Most were straightforward—*What is it about the weather you find so interesting? How did you recognize the impending tornado? Were those signs the same for the derecho? Can you describe the dangers of flash floods for our viewers?* and the like. But one question turned her blood to ice every time she read it.

Why were you in the lighthouse when the hurricane hit?

She couldn't tell Cheryl the truth. Doing so would break her promise to her father to keep Andy's secret. She'd gone around and around, trying to come up with a response to the question that wasn't an outright lie. The best she came up with was, *I was going for a bike ride and lost track of time. I took shelter in the lighthouse when it started to rain.*

Even that vague answer was problematic, though.

After all, she was a self-professed weather fanatic. Would she really have missed the warning signs of an approaching hurricane? Not likely. And what if people believed her answer? Her credibility as someone highly knowledgeable about the weather would fly right out the window. Was she willing to accept that outcome?

For Andy . . . yes. To save his reputation . . . yes.

But that night as she lay on a blanket in Fiesta Park, basking in the warm glow cast by hundreds of illuminated balloons tethered to the ground, she prayed that Cheryl would go off script and steer clear of that particular question.

"**H**ang on." Helicity stared at Cheryl's face on her phone screen, certain that she'd misunderstood what she'd just heard. "We're doing the interview from a *balloon*?"

Cheryl's eyes sparkled with delight beneath her baseball cap. "We are! I had to pull some strings, but it's all been arranged."

It was Sunday afternoon, and Helicity was in her bedroom getting ready for the upcoming interview. She'd styled her sandy-brown hair as best she could

and applied a layer of mascara to her lashes. The short-sleeve, forest-green dress that Mia, her personal fashion consultant, had declared "simple but sophisticated," hung on the back of the door. On the floor was the pair of strappy sandals Helicity had worn on her first—and only—date with Trey.

Cheryl gestured to someone out of frame. "George! Come meet Helicity. She's the girl I was telling you about."

A man stepped into view and whipped off his cowboy hat. His wide, toothy smile was overshadowed by a bushy brown mustache that matched his thick eyebrows. His face was leathery from years of sun exposure, his dark eyes sunken deep in wrinkles. But he radiated energy and enthusiasm. "Hope you're not afraid of heights, missy, because we are going to touch the sky!"

"George is our pilot," Cheryl explained. "He'll be in the air with us, obviously, along with my cameraman. Luckily, his gondola can carry eight people, so we'll have plenty of wiggle room. Right, George?"

"You know that's right, Cheryl! It's going to be beautiful, dramatic, awe-inspiring, you name it, your fans will love it. Now listen, Helicity, make sure you dress warm. The temperature up in the sky will be lots chillier than on the ground. And wear sneakers or boots because if we get blown off course—which we won't—and have to land in some thorny brush—which we won't—you'll want to have footwear that protects your tootsies."

Cheryl requested that they be at the balloon launch site by five o'clock sharp, then clicked off.

Helicity quickly texted Andy with the change in plans and then stared at herself in the bureau mirror. "You're going up in a balloon," she whispered. A smile crept over her face. "You're going to touch the sky."

Her smile turned wry when she glimpsed her outfit. *So much for simple and sophisticated,* she thought as she swapped the dress and the sandals for the clothes she'd worn on the plane: a pair of black leggings, a cobalt-blue T-shirt, and sneakers. At the last second, she grabbed a bulky sweatshirt, the only outerwear she'd brought.

"Guys have it so easy," she complained when Andy emerged in the kitchen after changing his khaki shorts for khaki pants.

"It's not what you wear, it's the confidence with which you wear it." He brushed off the front of his blue oxford shirt and swung a sweater borrowed from Mr. Bainbridge over his shoulder. "Didn't Mia ever tell you that?"

They arrived at the meeting site shortly before five. Helicity paused when she saw Cheryl. The talk-show host looked stylish in formfitting navy trousers and an oversize white cashmere sweater. Her auburn hair was fastened in a tidy side bun. Next to her, Helicity felt as put-together as a bag of dirty laundry.

"Hey." Lana appeared at her side. Over her arm was a well-worn leather jacket. She nodded at Helicity's sweatshirt. "Want to trade?"

Helicity slipped on the jacket with gratitude. It was warm and fit her like a glove. And from Sam's lingering look of approval, she gathered it did more for her appearance than the sweatshirt had.

She turned to watch their balloon being readied. Getting it aloft was no easy task. First, the ground crew spread out the brilliantly colored nylon balloon—or envelope, as Helicity learned it was called. Then they attached the wicker basket, or gondola, then moved to the top of the balloon to check the deflation port, used to release all the hot air upon landing, and the parachute valve used to slow a too-rapid ascent and aid a careful descent. Cold air was pumped into the envelope to inflate it. With the envelope quivering and fluttering on the ground like an enormous jellyfish, George stepped into the basket and fired the burner. Heat as intense as a flamethrower shot into the mouth of the balloon with a loud *whoosh*. Within seconds, the cold air heated up, and the envelope rose above them in its classic balloon shape.

It was all so enthralling, Helicity almost cheered.

Cheryl and another woman hurried over to Helicity and Andy while the crew ran through an extensive preflight checklist. While the woman pinned minuscule microphones to their lapels, Cheryl outlined the upcoming interviews.

"We'll start livestreaming when we leave the ground—get some fun coverage looking down as we ascend. We'll catch your reactions, too. And mine. I've never done this before, either! Once we're high enough, I'll start the interview. You'll both get a couple of softball questions to get you warmed up, and then we'll move on to the tornado and so forth. Just act like the camera isn't there and we're having a conversation. Getting to know each other. And smile. A smile always makes people feel at ease."

Behind them, George fired the burner again, sending out another blast of heat and sound. Cheryl grinned. "George has promised to give me a sign just before he has to do that so we can pause. But if a question or answer gets drowned out"—she shrugged— "hey, that's what puts the 'live' in 'livestreaming'!"

Her upbeat attitude was infectious. Any remaining nervousness Helicity had melted into excitement.

"Okeydokey, folks!" George called from the basket. "Time to get this show in the air!"

Helicity grabbed Andy's arm. "I can't believe we're doing this!"

"Yeah. I can't either."

She started. Her brother's voice, so lighthearted just an hour before, had turned subdued. His eyes were troubled. She glanced at Cheryl, who was chatting with her cameraman, then pulled Andy a few feet away. "Hey. You're okay with this, right?"

"The balloon ride, yes." He rubbed his hand across

his jaw. He'd nicked himself shaving earlier, and blood from the tiny cut left a smear on his chin. "What I'm going to say . . . I don't know."

She wiped away the smear with her thumb. "Do you want to back out?"

"Dunlaps! You ready?" Cheryl called to them from beside the balloon's basket.

Helicity ignored her. "You don't have to do this. I'll tell her you changed your mind."

He hesitated. "Will you still go through with it if I don't?"

Helicity nodded.

Andy looked over his shoulder at the balloon. "Okay. Then I'm going, too." But he didn't move and neither did she.

Helicity took hold of his hands then and looked him full in the face. "You know, according to Cheryl, going off script can be really satisfying. Just saying."

Something flickered behind his eyes. "Huh. Good to know."

Helicity gave his hands a squeeze. Then she let go and headed to the balloon. Her pulse raced as she stepped aboard. The gondola was divided into two sections, a small one for the pilot and the propane cylinders and another large enough for six people to stand with plenty of elbow room. The basket rocked slightly, but the ground crew had a firm hold on all sides, keeping it securely on the ground. Cheryl, Andy, and the cameraman climbed in after her. George shut and secured the basket's door and moved to the pilot section. Then he signaled his crew to let go and opened up a steady flame into the balloon.

With the heat flaring against her skin, her ears filled with the powerful blast of hot air, and her breath held tight in her lungs, Helicity looked away from the ground. Away from Sam and Lana and Ray and the Bainbridges and to the sky and the clouds and the lowering sun. She felt cloaked in serenity. Almost . . . worshipful.

Then the interview began.

heryl positioned herself in one corner of the rectangular basket. Helicity and Andy stood together facing her. The cameraman, a rangy twenty-something with a wedge of beard like a scuff mark on his chin, had been videoing over the side, but now slowly swiveled the camera up and around on its tripod so it was facing them and nodded at Cheryl.

"Hello, everyone!" Cheryl cried. "I'm Cheryl Wiggins, coming to you live from the International Balloon Fiesta in Albuquerque, New Mexico. Live . . .

and from a hot-air balloon owned and operated by pilot George Marks. Say hello, George!"

"Hello, George!" George repeated with a chortle of laughter.

Cheryl groaned. "One more bad joke like that, and I'll have Andy here toss you overboard."

Like the unblinking eye of a Cyclops, the camera panned toward Helicity and Andy. Cheryl moved closer until she was in the shot, too. "With me today are brother and sister Andy and Helicity Dunlap." Her expression morphed from welcoming to somber. "If you follow social media, you probably recognize their names. Maybe their faces, too. Not because of selfies they've posted or videos they've taken or anecdotes they've shared. No. In recent weeks, Helicity and Andy have been the unwilling subjects of online innuendo. Stories about them, stories rooted in mean-spirited, hateful, and hurtful gossip, have gone viral."

Beside the cameraman, George raised his arm. Cheryl paused while he fired the burner.

"As my loyal viewers know," she resumed, "my show strives to celebrate and uplift, not insult and embarrass." She pressed her lips together and narrowed her eyes. "So, imagine my dismay when I learned that a recent interview of mine was generating negative comments about Helicity."

Helicity listened to Cheryl recap the interview with Charles Bainbridge. "I won't speculate on how Helicity's selfless act became the object of online ridicule. To do so would be to mimic her critics' approach. Instead, I'll let her speak for herself. About the hurricane, yes, and about her other experiences with severe weather as well. But I want to drill deeper than that and get to know her as a *person*. I think you'll be surprised, delighted even, by what you learn about her." She smiled warmly at Helicity. "I know I was when I first met her."

She paused again for George to send another blast of heat into the balloon. Helicity marveled at the gentleness with which they rose higher into the air. She'd imagined it would be a jerkier motion, like when an elevator accelerated upward. She appreciated the momentary quiet that followed the blast, too, when she could clearly hear voices and music and laughter wafting up from the crowds down below. Tabitha's voice suddenly rang out above them all.

"That's my greatest friend Helicity on TV!"

Cheryl chuckled. "Seems I'm not the only one who likes you, Helicity." She nodded at the camera. "Go ahead. Say hi to your friends on the ground. Both of you!"

Helicity and Andy waved. "Hi, Tabitha! Hi, Sam! Hi, Lana and Ray and Mr. Bainbridge!" she said, earning a distant whoop in response from those below.

"And hi to Mom and Dad, too!" Andy added, nudging her reproachfully.

"Oh, yeah. And Mia and Trey and Suze!" Helicity put in.

Cheryl smiled. "All right. Before we get into all you've been through these past few months, Helicity, I'd like to know a little more about your history with the weather." She leaned in. "How long have you been fascinated by storms?"

Cheryl had instructed them to direct their replies to her, not the camera. So Helicity did her best to ignore the faint whir of the lens as it zoomed in closer to her. Still, knowing she was being videoed gave her a sudden bout of nerves that made her voice crack. She cleared her throat and tried again. "It's not just storms,

Cheryl," she finally managed to say. "It's everything about the weather. Although I guess my interest did start with a storm."

Cheryl nodded encouragingly.

"I was three years old," Helicity continued, "when a really big thunderstorm knocked out our electricity for hours." She glanced at Andy. "Remember that?"

He nodded. "Mom, Dad, and I played games by flashlight, then by candlelight when the batteries burned out. Not you, though. You ran from window to window, hoping to see more lightning. You tried to count the raindrops, even though you could only count to ten." He grinned. "You didn't cry when the thunder boomed. You cried when it stopped."

"And the next time we were at the library," Helicity said, picking up the story, "I made Mom take out every picture book on the weather I could find. For a long time, my favorite was *Cloudy with a Chance of Meatballs*."

Andy groaned. "I remember reading that to you. Over and over and over."

"Mom was so psyched when I learned to read," Helicity said with a laugh. "After that, I pretty much devoured any book about the weather I could get my hands on."

"Why did you—do you—find weather so intriguing?" Cheryl prompted.

"It's a lot of things, I guess." Helicity spread her hands wide. "The fact that it touches every single person on the planet. No matter who they are or where they live or what they do, some part of their day will be impacted by rain or wind or sun or snow or freezing cold or blasting heat—"

With perfect comedic timing, George fired the burner. He grinned sheepishly when Cheryl shot him a mock-warning look. She shook her head and indicated Helicity should continue.

"I like that the weather can't be controlled or changed. If it's going to snow, it's going to snow. Nothing we can do about it, even though we know why it's happening." Helicity rushed on, gesticulating with her hands as she warmed to her subject. "It's the *why* that really grabs me, though. Why sometimes dark clouds dump inches of rain in an hour and other times they move off without releasing a single drop. Why a tropical storm out in the Atlantic sometimes grows into a hurricane and other times fizzles and dies. Why clouds can look wispy or menacing or even like a line of waves on the ocean. Why certain wind, air, and moisture conditions cause tornadoes and waterspouts to spin up. Why lakes generate big blizzards one winter and only spit snowflakes the next." She grinned and, with a sweep of her arm, looked toward the nearby mountains and valley on the horizon. "Why a phenomenon like the Albuquerque Box . . ."

Her voice trailed off as something caught her eye.

"Helicity?" Cheryl prodded. "You were telling our viewers about the Albuquerque Box?"

Helicity continued to stare at the valley. Something was different down there. But what? A sudden puff of air tossed her hair into her eyes. She pushed it away impatiently and focused again on the valley. Then she looked up at the sky. Not the sky directly overhead, but just beyond the same patch of valley.

Andy touched her arm. "Hel? Everything okay?"

Helicity shook her head, perplexed. Without taking her eyes off the valley, she called to the pilot. "George, what was the forecast for today?"

"Slight chance of thunderstorms, but nowhere near us. Why?"

Helicity frowned. She could see dark clouds farther back on the horizon, but what she was seeing closer to Fiesta Park didn't look like a thunderstorm. It was much lower to the ground than a storm would be. And the clouds were the wrong color. Not gray and white, but reddish orange. She wished she had binoculars to see them better. Then she remembered an old trick to help bring objects in the distance into clearer focus. She curled her hands into circles and held them to one eye like a telescope.

What she saw through her cupped fingers made her blood freeze. She whipped around, her mouth gaping like a fish.

"My God, Hel! What is it? What's wrong?" Andy cried.

She croaked out one word around the terror closing her throat: *"Haboob!"*

CHAPTER TWENTY-THREE

For one heart-stopping second, nobody moved or said anything. Then a blaring alarm from a phone broke the spell. Helicity reached for her back pocket before remembering that she and Andy had left their phones behind per Cheryl's instruction.

George still had his, though. "My God," he said, scanning the screen. "She's right. A massive dust storm just blew up north of the park." He looked up, his leathery face a mask of fear. "And it's coming straight toward us."

While he was speaking, more blares, thousands of them, fainter and discordant and never ending, sounded from below. A cacophony of voices laced with terror rose through the air. Andy, Helicity, and Cheryl gripped the edge of the basket and stared down. The cameraman abandoned his equipment and gawked at the scene below, too. George stayed by the tanks, but like the others, his gaze was on the chaos erupting on the ground.

Crowds of panicked spectators surged like an incoming tide toward the two park exits. Almost immediately, the bottleneck effect made by so many people trying to funnel through the small spaces at the same time slowed them to a standstill.

Andy clutched the wicker basket. "Will they make it to their cars in time?"

"I hope so," Helicity said. She looked from the people to the reddish cloud. "Because if the haboob catches them . . ." She bit her lip and shook her head.

"Forget about them," the cameraman cried. "What about us? We're right in its path!" He whirled on George. "What are you waiting for? You're the pilot! Steer us out of the way!"

"You can't steer a balloon," George said tightly. "But I can get us down." He moved for the parachute valve cord. One tug and air would start escaping through a vent at the top of the envelope, moving the balloon slowly downward.

Downward and into the path of the oncoming storm. "George, wait! Don't!" Helicity shouted.

George froze. The cameraman glared at Helicity. "Don't listen to her! If you can get us down, do it!"

Helicity lunged forward over the basket divide, accidentally knocking the camera sideways, and grabbed George's arm by the sleeve to stop him. Still holding on, she glared back at the cameraman. "That haboob is coming at us at fifty miles an hour or more. We start to descend, and we could be caught in dust so thick we won't be able to see or breathe." She glanced at George. "You want to try landing in something like that?"

George blanched and shook his head. She turned back to the cameraman. "And it won't be just dust that's clogging your eyes, nose, mouth, and lungs. That wind carries airborne bacteria, viruses, and fungi. You breathe that stuff in and you'll be coughing it up for days. And years from now, when you're lying in bed wasting away from some kind of pulmonary disease, you'll wonder which of those pathogens caused your sickness. And that's if—*if*—we survive a landing in winds gusting more than sixty miles an hour. *That's* why I told George to wait."

That shut the cameraman up for a moment. Then he hissed, "You got all the answers? Fine. You tell us what to do. And it's on your head if it all goes wrong."

"I can live with that." Helicity turned away from him. "George, how high can this balloon go?"

He stared at her uncomprehendingly.

"How high?" she demanded.

"The highest I've ever done is six thousand feet."

Helicity nodded. "Okay. Okay. That should be enough. Take us up to that height."

"The winds could be much stronger up there," George warned.

"Will you still be able to control the balloon?"

He ran his hand through his hair. "I'll do my best."

"Good. Take us up. Now."

"Why?"

Helicity started. Andy had been so silent she'd

almost forgotten he was there. "Why?" he repeated.

"Haboobs typically reach heights of three thousand feet," she informed him. "If we get up high enough, we might be able to ride it out above the worst of the dust and wind."

Andy nodded. "Then we should tell the others."

Helicity blinked, not sure who he meant. Then she remembered that they were not alone in the skies. A dozen other balloons were circling on the Albuquerque Box currents. "The other pilots. Can we contact them?"

"My radio." George thrust the device into Andy's hands and ran through a quick explanation on how to broadcast a message to the other pilots. At the same time, he turned a knob on the propane line connected to the burner, increasing the flow of fuel. When he ignited the propane, a towering column of fire much larger and hotter than any previous burns shot into the envelope. As they ascended steadily, flames from other balloons flared, telling Helicity that Andy's message had been received and understood.

"All those people." Cheryl was still staring at the rapidly retreating ground. Her face was streaked with

CHAPTER TWENTY-FOUR

Those twenty minutes were some of the longest in Helicity's life. She and Andy huddled together, staring down at the ground far, far below. At some point, the temporary plastic fences surrounding Fiesta Park had been torn down—by park employees desperate to help or frantic spectators, Helicity didn't know. But the tactic worked. The field was clear of people when the dust storm blew in. She gasped as the parking lots disappeared beneath the enormous cloud, obliterating the cars and RVs and

tears. "Some are taking cover in the park buildings. But will they be safe there from the wind and dust?"

"Safer than they would be outside," Helicity replied. She closed her eyes. Terrifying pictures played through her mind. Of Ray and Lana, Sam and Tabitha and Mr. Bainbridge, lost in the mob below. Struggling to get to safety before the dust storm consumed them. Fighting to survive. Of Scout, waiting at home for Tabitha. Of her parents clutching each other as the livestream abruptly ended.

A change in the air made her open her eyes again. The haboob had blown closer, bowing outward in an arc like a roll of dough pushed forward at its middle. She stared down at the billowing mass, horror-struck and yet fascinated. Her brain conjured up everything she knew about the giant dust storms. They were born from updrafts of air hot enough to prevent rain from reaching the ground. That same rain cooled the air suddenly. The cool air dropped in a stronger-than-normal downdraft, and the downdraft blew a gust front. In areas where the surface terrain was more dust than dirt, the gust front churned up a wide cloud of thick, choking particulates thousands of feet high. The cloud could travel for several miles, coating everything and everyone in a powdery layer, before finally dissipating.

And there was nothing anybody could do to stop it. They could only get out of its way. Shelter in cars or buildings. Wait for it to blow over, for the dust to settle, for the damage to be done.

"Five thousand feet," George informed them over the roar of the flames. Then a short time later, "Five thousand five hundred."

But just as Helicity allowed herself to hope that her plan would work, George twisted the propane knob again. The flame weakened from a blazing column to a sputtering cone.

"What'd you do that for?" the cameraman shouted. He stabbed a finger at Helicity. "She said six thousand feet!"

George washed his face with his hands. "Yeah, well, it's gonna be zero feet real soon if I don't cut back."

"What? Why?"

He tapped the fuel gauge. "Because burning hot like that uses a lot of fuel. We started with enough for an easy hour of low-level drifting. Now I reckon we

have about twenty minutes left b[...] descending."

"And if we run out of propane [...] the ground?" Cheryl asked.

George raised a fist and slamme[...] open palm with a loud smack. "We f[...] of potatoes."

trucks from view. It swept over the grassy field, gusting and rolling and billowing for what felt like hours, but turned out to be a few minutes.

Then the haboob moved on, heading south.

"What else is in its way?" Cheryl asked George. She seemed dazed, a hollow shell drained of energy.

"Neighborhoods. A Little League field. An industrial complex. Beyond that . . ." He shook his head.

They drifted northward in silence after that, the only sound coming from the flame. Then George cleared his throat.

"It's now or never." He caught Helicity's eye and indicated the propane line with an inclination of his head. "Are we good?"

She checked the ground again. The air was starting to clear, like fog lifting at dawn, revealing a park that had been transformed into an alien landscape. The green grass was tarnished a red orange hue. Lumpen shapes—abandoned balloons and baskets, buildings, tents, lawn chairs, and vendors' stalls—stood out like warts on smooth skin. If they'd tried landing before the storm . . . She shook her head. They hadn't. And her plan to outlast the haboob by riding above it had succeeded. What they'd face when they set down, though . . .

"We're good," she told George.

The descent was eerily peaceful, the sound of the envelope deflating like a long, gentle sigh. As they neared the surface, George warned them that without a ground crew, the landing would be very rough. "Be ready to brace for impact."

He needn't have worried. A handful of men and women in park uniforms rushed out from nearby buildings. Bandanas covered their mouths and noses, making them look like a swarm of bandits. Dust billowed up in angry whorls around them, their feet kicking up in choking puffs. The cameraman shot Helicity an alarmed look, no doubt remembering her description of the dust's hazards.

"Like this!" She buried her nose and mouth in the crook of her elbow. The others immediately did the same, narrowing their eyes against the particulates at the same time.

With his free hand, George activated the deflator port to release the last of the balloon's air. They descended rapidly, the surface winds pushing them tears. "Some are taking cover in the park buildings. But will they be safe there from the wind and dust?"

"Safer than they would be outside," Helicity replied. She closed her eyes. Terrifying pictures played through her mind. Of Ray and Lana, Sam and Tabitha and Mr. Bainbridge, lost in the mob below. Struggling to get to safety before the dust storm consumed them. Fighting to survive. Of Scout, waiting at home for Tabitha. Of her parents clutching each other as the livestream abruptly ended.

A change in the air made her open her eyes again. The haboob had blown closer, bowing outward in an arc like a roll of dough pushed forward at its middle. She stared down at the billowing mass, horror-struck and yet fascinated. Her brain conjured up everything she knew about the giant dust storms. They were born from updrafts of air hot enough to prevent rain from reaching the ground. That same rain cooled the air suddenly. The cool air dropped in a stronger-than-normal downdraft, and the downdraft blew a gust front. In areas where the surface terrain was more dust than dirt, the gust front churned up a wide cloud of thick, choking particulates thousands of feet high. The cloud could travel for several miles, coating everything and everyone in a powdery layer, before finally dissipating.

And there was nothing anybody could do to stop it. They could only get out of its way. Shelter in cars or buildings. Wait for it to blow over, for the dust to settle, for the damage to be done.

"Five thousand feet," George informed them over the roar of the flames. Then a short time later, "Five thousand five hundred."

But just as Helicity allowed herself to hope that her plan would work, George twisted the propane knob again. The flame weakened from a blazing column to a sputtering cone.

"What'd you do that for?" the cameraman shouted. He stabbed a finger at Helicity. "She said six thousand feet!"

George washed his face with his hands. "Yeah, well, it's gonna be zero feet real soon if I don't cut back."

"What? Why?"

He tapped the fuel gauge. "Because burning hot like that uses a lot of fuel. We started with enough for an easy hour of low-level drifting. Now I reckon we have about twenty minutes left before we need to start descending."

"And if we run out of propane before we make it to the ground?" Cheryl asked.

George raised a fist and slammed it down into his open palm with a loud smack. "We free-fall like a sack of potatoes."

CHAPTER TWENTY-FOUR

Those twenty minutes were some of the longest in Helicity's life. She and Andy huddled together, staring down at the ground far, far below. At some point, the temporary plastic fences surrounding Fiesta Park had been torn down—by park employees desperate to help or frantic spectators, Helicity didn't know. But the tactic worked. The field was clear of people when the dust storm blew in. She gasped as the parking lots disappeared beneath the enormous cloud, obliterating the cars and RVs and trucks from view. It swept over the grassy field, gusting and rolling and billowing for what felt like hours, but turned out to be a few minutes.

Then the haboob moved on, heading south.

"What else is in its way?" Cheryl asked George. She seemed dazed, a hollow shell drained of energy.

"Neighborhoods. A Little League field. An industrial complex. Beyond that . . ." He shook his head.

They drifted northward in silence after that, the only sound coming from the flame. Then George cleared his throat.

"It's now or never." He caught Helicity's eye and indicated the propane line with an inclination of his head. "Are we good?"

She checked the ground again. The air was starting to clear, like fog lifting at dawn, revealing a park that had been transformed into an alien landscape. The green grass was tarnished a red orange hue. Lumpen shapes—abandoned balloons and baskets, buildings, tents, lawn chairs, and vendors' stalls—stood out like warts on smooth skin. If they'd tried landing before the storm . . . She shook her head. They hadn't. And her plan to outlast the haboob by riding above it had succeeded. What they'd face when they set down, though . . .

"We're good," she told George.

The descent was eerily peaceful, the sound of the envelope deflating like a long, gentle sigh. As they neared the surface, George warned them that without a ground crew, the landing would be very rough. "Be ready to brace for impact."

He needn't have worried. A handful of men and women in park uniforms rushed out from nearby buildings. Bandanas covered their mouths and noses, making them look like a swarm of bandits. Dust billowed up in angry whorls around them, their feet kicking up in choking puffs. The cameraman shot Helicity an alarmed look, no doubt remembering her description of the dust's hazards.

"Like this!" She buried her nose and mouth in the crook of her elbow. The others immediately did the same, narrowing their eyes against the particulates at the same time.

With his free hand, George activated the deflator port to release the last of the balloon's air. They descended rapidly, the surface winds pushing them sideways at an awkward angle. Before they hit the ground, three park workers caught hold of the gondola, stopped its motion, and guided it down. Two others grabbed a line dangling down from the top of the envelope and tugged the deflated balloon until it lay flat on the ground like an enormous dead fish.

As they scurried, one of the men pressed a bandana into Helicity's hand. She quickly tied it around her nose and mouth. Andy and the others did the same. Then the same man grasped Helicity's hand and shook it. "You were amazing. Truly."

Helicity blinked against the blowing dust that collected in her lashes and eyes. "I—what?" she asked, her voice muffled beneath the cloth.

The man pointed to the camera. It was still mounted on its tripod, though it was tilted sideways over the gondola and pointed downward. It was still livestreaming footage, even now. "We didn't see much more than glimpses of what was happening. But we heard everything you said. So we know."

"Know what?"

"You saved them, Helicity." He looked past her

shoulder, tears pooling in his eyes. She turned to see other balloons floating downward toward the Mars-scape surface, other crews swarming to help them land amid the dust, other pilots and passengers pausing to look her way.

"You saved them all."

Helicity had no memory of how she got from the park to the Bainbridges' house. One moment she was standing on the field. The next, Lana was wrapping her arms around her and not letting go.

Tabitha and Mr. Bainbridge had been safe from harm the whole time, Helicity learned after a hot shower and two phone calls, one with Andy to their parents and one to Mia. Rather than watch the live feed on their phones in the park, they had returned to the Bainbridges' house to watch in air-conditioned comfort on TV.

"It missed us completely," Mr. Bainbridge said in disbelief. "Not even a dusting here."

Helicity nodded. She knew from firsthand experience that storms that razed one area could leave another just a few miles—even a few feet—away untouched.

Lana, Ray, and Sam had been at the Bainbridges', too. But when the phone alert came, their itch to chase the storm sent them clambering into Mo West. "We caught some footage and sent out a few of our remote-sensing drones to record the conditions of the atmosphere surrounding that beast," Ray informed Helicity with satisfaction. "Coupled with what your camera got, even at its crazy angle, we have a great deal of information about this particular haboob."

"And I got some interesting photos," Sam added. He waggled his eyebrows. "Maybe you'd like one?"

Lana said nothing. But her smile, the sparkle in her eyes, sent Helicity a clear message: *The sun is emerging from behind the clouds.*

Mr. Bainbridge was rummaging in his kitchen, trying to rustle up something for dinner, when Cheryl and George arrived unexpectedly with pizza for everyone. The cameraman, whose name Helicity never did learn, wasn't with them. Helicity wasn't terribly disappointed by his absence.

After everyone had eaten, Andy stood up and

clinked his glass with a spoon to get their attention. "I was going to make a big speech," he said. "Something deep and meaningful that would have you all in tears. But I think I'll keep it simple instead." He looked at his sister, a lopsided smile on his face, and raised his glass. "To Helicity."

"To Helicity!" they all echoed lustily.

Flushing with equal parts pleasure and embarrassment, she buried her nose in Scout's fur. But her eyes shone at Andy.

The gathering broke up soon afterward. As Helicity waved good-bye to Cheryl and George, she wondered if she'd ever hear from the television host again.

She did—less than an hour later, in fact.

For what it's worth, Cheryl's text read, *social media loves you right now. Andy, too.*

Helicity knew she should be happy about that. But mostly, she wanted to forget about posts and selfies and comments and viral videos. Well, for a while, anyway.

Then it was time for Sam, Lana, and Ray to head back to Ray's family's house. Helicity hugged them each in turn. When she got to Lana, she tried to give back the leather jacket. Lana refused to take it. "When you wear it, remember how strong you are."

She embraced Sam last. He pulled back after a moment. Just far enough so his mouth hovered over hers. Close enough so she could look deep into his eyes, feel her heart bump against his chest. But when he leaned in to kiss her, she stopped him with a finger on his lips.

"It's too much," she whispered. "Right now . . . it's too much."

He searched her eyes. Then he nodded once, climbed into Mo West, and was gone.

Inside, she spotted Andy out by the pool. She sank down onto the lounge chair beside him. They sat in silence in the flickering light of the moon on the water.

"I was going to do it." Andy's voice was soft but earnest. "Tell Cheryl, I mean. My story. My *whole* story."

Helicity turned her head to look at him. "Hey." He looked back. "I believe you."

They were quiet for a few more minutes. Then Andy broke the silence again. "How do you do it, Hel? Everything you've been through . . . how do you keep going?"

She tilted her head back and stared at the stars. "Simple." She captured her necklace. Slid her fingers to the charms. Held the lightning bolt.

"I'm a survivor."

ACKNOWLEDGMENTS

All through school, math and science were "my subjects," but I did love to write. After I switched schools in seventh grade I had a teacher tell me that "maybe writing wasn't my thing."

I let that label stay with me as I became a scientist and even into the early part of my career.

I went to see Wendy Lefkon at Disney • Hyperion to pitch a baby board book—but I figured I could handle sixty words or so—she encouraged me to try writing for middle grade. I sent her some ideas and she said, that's great, let's do a trilogy. My "not a writer" label was immediately reversed. I want to thank you, Wendy, for believing in me. And major thanks to Stephanie Peters for teaching me the voice of a middle grade reader.

This series would not have been possible without the support of my husband, Ben, my boys, Adrian and Miles, and my parents for always encouraging me to dream.

And to Helicity—the name I told my husband I wanted to give a daughter if we had one (I think Ben was pleased we didn't have to use my "nerd glossary" to name our child), but with this final book complete, I feel like I have a daughter in Helicity. And I truly hope it's not the end of her adventure.